KILLER'S CURSE

WENDY H. JONES

SCOTT AND LAWSON

COPYRIGHT

DEDICATION

To Valerie Dickinson who won a charity auction to have her name used as a character in a book. Valerie, I hope you are happy with your character.

A robin trilled, the only sound disturbing the otherwise tranquil scene. A thin layer of snow carpeted the woods in a glittering white blanket and coated the bare, skeletonised, branches of the surrounding trees. Tiny icicles hung in a sparkling curtain - a myriad of festive ornaments ready for the Christmas season. Nature displayed its glorious winter beauty.

The robin's breast wasn't the only red to be found in the woods that day. Red - the colour of rage, the colour of death and, conversely, the Chinese colour for luck, happiness and good fortune. The bodies lying on the ground, an equal pairing, wore clothes of scarlet, a colour mimicked by the blood that stained the otherwise pristine snow. Red hadn't brought them much luck.

Three red candles, precisely placed around each head, formed an ecclesiastical halo of imaginary light. A finishing touch, without which the scene would be incomplete.

Fat flakes of soft snow fell softly, silently, to the ground. Another, then another, quickly forming into a whirling maelstrom of white, hiding the fleeing figure from sight and deadening the sound of their steps; a silent accomplice to the murderous deed it had just observed. The scene returned to nature, the bodies at one with the landscape, as snow hid them from sight.

Tranquillity is often merely an illusion.

"First Nuns, then vicars and now - wait for it - Santas. You're a wee bit peculiar when it comes tae deid bodies, Ma'am."

"Peter, I swear, if you don't speak English, yours will be the next dead body." DI Shona McKenzie gazed down at the brace of corpses lying at her feet. Mr and Mrs Claus by the looks of their apparel. She could just picture the field day the local rag, otherwise known as *The Courier,* would have with that one. She shivered at the thought. Or was it the cold. Difficult to tell. She pulled her scarf tighter and her beanie hat further down. Difficult under swathes of white material, otherwise known as a crime scene coverall. Finishing the adjustments, she peered around just in case Adanna Okifor leapt out from behind a tree. Dark skinned and perpetually happy, the reporter seemed to be everywhere. Everywhere Shona's cases were, that is. Okifor could smell out a story like a ferret after a rabbit. A stunningly beautiful ferret but that didn't change the outcome.

Shona dragged her wandering thoughts back to the case. Templeton Woods had seen more than its fair share of murders, but this was the creepiest yet. This took some doing, as her cases usually tended to the crazier side of murder. These bodies were fully clothed with their hats still firmly in place. Nothing abnormal about that at first glance. However, what wasn't in place was their heads. Chopped from the torsos they lay neatly next to them. One head sported long auburn hair, the other white snowy locks and a flowing beard. Could be the real deal when it came to Father Christmas.

"If the press reports this we'll have kids wailing from here to Wick and back, then onwards tae the Borders."

"What do you mean if? Actually, they won't." She glared at Peter to emphasise her point. "This is one time when the freedom of the press is going to be shut down quicker than you can say Santa."

"I'll help you close them." Fighting talk from a man who thought *The Courier* should be elevated and put on a pedestal, alongside the bust of Johan Carolus, who printed the first ever newspaper - in the world. *The Courier* and its sister publication, *The Dundee Evening Telegraph,* were the very pinnacle of journalists according to her sergeant. Obviously, Christmas meant more to him than his favoured oracle of all things Dundee news. Go figure. Shona's views on the press were less favourable. They tended more to the 'miserable bunch of useless tossers' end of the spectrum. She also thought Johan Carolus should be consigned to hell with the fires stoked high, using copies of every newspaper ever written.

"What have you got against journalism anyway, Ma'am? You never did say." Peter obviously woke up fearless that morning.

"Mind your own beeswax." Her tone mild all things considered, Shona glared at him.

Peter smiled. He'd ferret it out of her sometime or another.

"What's with the candles, Peter?" Shona pointed with her toe. "Are candle halos some sort of strange Dundee ritual?"

"No' that I'm aware of. We're usually the kill and leave type of murder. Might be a wee finishing touch because it's Christmas."

"Great. Now we've got a killer who thinks he's an artist. God only knows what we'll get next."

"I hope they dinnae start on the nativity as a follow up," The sergeant's voice sounded a little too cheery for the macabre words.

"Don't jinx things." Shona's heart sank, despite her words. She really hoped this would not be the case. A serial killer targeting Christmas was the last thing she needed.

Shoving aside thoughts of the press, which only depressed her, Shona focussed on the task at hand. Headless Claus's were unusual, even in her orbit. She was only glad there were no Claus Juniors involved. This was one shout she dreaded. Fortunately, she had mercifully avoided murders involving children so far in her career.

"How come there are only two of us investigating this? What's happened to the rest of the team?"

Peter glanced around and lifted an enquiring eyebrow. There were enough officers milling about to fill a small stadium.

Shona caught the look. "You know what I mean. Are the rest of the team having a little lay in? Don't fancy coming to work today?"

The words had barely left her mouth when four bodies came hurtling towards her.

"Sorry, Ma'am." DC Roy MacGregor rocked the look you'd expect for a wild night out.

"Car trouble," said Detective Sergeant Abigail Lau, a smile lighting up her Asian features, giving her a startling beauty. "I had to pick this lot up as they'd be over the limit.

"She drives like an old woman." Detective Sergeant Nina

Chakrabarti was dressed head to toe in designer clothes and a disgusted look.

Jason Roberts, the final member of Shona's team, said nothing. He came to this momentous decision after one look at the DI's face. The DI who was currently shouting, "Come one step closer to my crime scene and your dead bodies will be cheering me up no end."

Four bodies screeched to a halt. Frozen in place as though in response to the weather itself.

"Get yourselves covered up. Destroy one bit of evidence and this team will be four members short."

Their about turn couldn't be quicker if they'd done it on a carousel.

Roy returned first, with a haste not seen since the retreat of the Light Brigade. Taking in the sight at his feet his jaw dropped even faster. "Is that Father Christmas and his missus?" he asked. "Seriously, Ma'am, you don't half attract them."

The others joined them, suited up and ready for action. A full quota of Dundee's finest detectives. Shona sometimes wondered about the finest part but tended to give them the benefit of the doubt.

"DC MacGregor, keep your opinions to yourself." The look she gave him could freeze an Eskimo's gonads. "Keep things professional or I'll professionally remove you from the case and into a post which will have you chained to the chief's side for the rest of your natural."

"What I really meant to say was, I'm excited we have another case which will take us into the realms of impossibility." He bit his lip, then continued, "I love a challenge."

"I'm more worried it will be Rudolph next. If an animal dies, we're toast," said PC Iain Barrow, the team's photographer and hot shot evidence collector. He'd joined them, seemingly from nowhere.

Shona inwardly agreed. The human psyche could just about cope with dead humans, but dead animals were a whole different herd of reindeer. "Where have you been. Having a wee nap?"

"Nope, I was here first. Took some photos and then did a perimeter sweep."

Shona's mouth opened. Before she got one word in, Iain said, "I cleared it with SOCO."

Shona grinned. "Top man." She gazed around her, taking in a team who were still standing around like lemons. "Maybe you lot might want to follow Iain's example and search the scene. If it's not too much trouble of course." Sarcasm dropped from every well pronounced syllable.

Amongst mutters of, "Brown noser," they all set to and formed a tight search party. Shona smiled, heartened they were now working together rather than at each other's throats. God only knows, it took them long enough, she supposed. A closely-knit team they definitely were not but as each case progressed the general ambience and bonhomie improved. By the time she retired they might all like each other. Shona remained ever the optimist.

W hilst this witty repartee unfolded, Detective Sergeant Peter Johnston surveyed the scene with a well-practiced eye, simultaneously slapping together hands the size of shovels. Shona's sergeant could never be described as dainty. Stamping feet accompanied the hand slapping.

"How come the eejits can't wait until summer to kill off the population."

"If you're referring to the good citizens of Dundee, who the heck knows." Shona's shrug could barely be seen under the layer of clothes. "Any season seems to be the perfect time for murder around here."

They peered at the scene as if concentration would magic up an answer written in twelve-foot letters in the snow.

Shona dragged her gaze back to Peter. "Who found them?"

"A grave digger taking a shortcut to Birkhill Cemetery."

"A shortcut? Where on earth from? We're in the middle of nowhere." Shona's thoughts wandered to their previous cases involving these woods. They'd seen more than their fair share of murders and her toes curled at the thought of walking through them in the gloom of an early winter morning.

Peter chose to take the path of least resistance to her words and ignored both the sarcasm and gross exaggeration. "If you'd like a wee chat with him, he's in a nice warm police car." Peter knew his inspector well.

At this heart-warming thought she nodded her head, swivelled, and put one sodden foot in front of the other, in the direction of their witness. She untied the hood of her white suit as she went, making sure she was well outside the crime scene first. POLSA, lovely man that he was, would have her guts for shoelaces if she contaminated the area. Much as she liked to think it was her crime scene, everyone, including her, knew the truth. POLSA allowed her the privilege of appearing to be in charge. For this, he was at the top of her very short Christmas card list. Not many people made it on the list in the first instance. She had better things to worry her than fancy cards. Dead bodies for example.

Her toes started to thaw as she interviewed the suspect who was, indeed, tucked up, nice and warm, in a police car. His name was Archie Greenlove and he lived in an old farm cottage behind the woods. This really was a shortcut to his place of work, which came as a revelation to Shona. After three years, she still discovered things daily about her new home city.

"I've a grave tae dig." Archie's green eyes darted everywhere, as though planning an escape. "There's a funeral due and nae grave." He paused and took a few faltering breaths. "My boss'll no' like it."

Shona gently touched his hand. "What's your boss's number? I'll ring him."

"I cannae lose my job. The wife's not well." As he spoke,

Archie pulled a notebook from his pocket. His gnarled fingers flicked a few pages and he slowly read out a number.

"Thanks." Shona tapped the digits out on her screen, spoke into the phone and pressed end. "He's sorting it."

If anything, Archie's face was greyer than before she'd made the call. Obviously, his imminent job loss wasn't the worst of his worries. The darting eyes had been joined by trembling limbs.

Shona thought he'd be used to dead bodies in his line of work. Although most of the deceased he came across were probably tidily inside a casket, not lying around with their heads detached. She reached across and held his hand. "I know it's a shock and I really understand that. The best thing you can do to help those poor souls now, is tell us everything you know. We'll need to record this." She pulled a voice recorder from her pocket. The size of a cigarette lighter it could record several interviews and still have room for a couple of novels. Shona marvelled at the way modern technology was going.

Archie nodded his consent to the recording. After a few false starts, he took a deep breath and mustered up the courage to keep going. "My car widnae start so I had tae walk to the cemetery. The quickest way's through the woods." He faltered, gave a slight shake of his body, and started again. "I'm never going inside those woods again." His eyes grew vacant.

"What happened next?" Shona's gentle voice cut through his internal dialogue.

"Something caught my eye. Red. Thought the youngsters who make out here might have left a coat."

Good grief, thought Shona, who would want to make out in murder central? In the middle of winter? There's no curing stupid, or cupid, she supposed.

"Then I saw the santas. And the heads." He swallowed. "And the blood." More swallowing. Shona thought he might throw up but he managed to pull himself together. "So, I ran out of the woods and phoned you lot." The last words came out in a rush and a jumble. His breathing quickened.

"Nice slow breaths. In and out. In and out." The last thing Shona wanted was the witness passing out. Didn't help the interview much and the paperwork would keep her buried until Easter.

Archie complied and a tinge of pink returned to his cheeks.

Letting out a breath she didn't realise she was holding; Shona gave him a minute to compose himself. "Did you see anything? Anything at all?"

He threw her an 'are you addled' type of look. "I was that shook up, I wisnae looking for clues. Is that no' your job?"

"It is. I assure you my officers are doing their level best to hunt for them as we speak. We still need eagled-eyed witnesses such as yourself though." Shona groaned inwardly at what she'd just said. "Did you see footsteps? Dogs? People?"

"I'd love to help you, Hen, but I was late for work and once I saw those bodies, I ran."

"Thanks for your help, Mr. Greenlove. One of my officers will drive you to the station and we'll get your statement in writing." Shona switched off the voice recorder and shoved it deep in an inside pocket.

"Can I have a cuppy tea when I get tae Bell Street. My nerves are shot."

"I'll make sure of it." Bell Street, the main station in Dundee, was unimaginatively named after the street in which it was built. It had housed a veritable plethora of murderers since the opening ribbon was cut over a hundred years previously. Including, allegedly, Jack the Ripper. Shona thought it would see many more if she took her current case into consideration. She shoved the car door open and slipped out into the icy blast, pulling her hood up as she went. The white suit blended with the snow, making her at one with the elements.

11

4

Shona's mood lightened by several shades as she approached the scene of the crime. This had more to do with the fact her fiancé was now in attendance than anything to do with moving the case forward. The Procurator Fiscal, Douglas Lawson, also happened to be the love of Shona's life. He and Peter were currently gazing at her brace of corpses.

"Douglas, what a lovely surprise." Her voice was far warmer than it should have been given the seriousness of the task in hand.

He swivelled around and grinned. "Here we go again, Shona. You're hard at it, increasing Dundee's body count on what seems like a daily basis. Nary a one and then you turn up and bingo." He grinned.

"You obviously feel like being an ex-fiancé." The warmth in her voice dropped several degrees. She'd had it to the back teeth with ribbing about the city's high body count. Add that to the fact she'd be answering to said body count in front of her boss's desk later and she was not a happy Inspector.

"Noted. What have we got?"

"Two bodies and not a clue is what we've got."

"Situation normal then. Have we had a police surgeon to declare them?"

"Nope, although I think we can safely say they're dead."

"Protocol, Dear Lady." Douglas grinned and took a step back.

"Call me that again and you might find yourself suddenly single again."

Douglas saluted, his grin lighting up the dismal scene.

Their faces soon turned serious as a small whirlwind approached. This was Whitney, the new Police Surgeon, whizzing toward them in her usual excitable fashion. Screeching to a halt, she took one look at the bodies and said, "And you needed me, why?"

"The PF insists it's protocol."

"Cannae upset the Fiscal. He's the fount o' all knowledge in all things criminal." Peter tipped his head in Douglas's direction.

"Well, I can assure you the bodies are dead. My medical degree wasn't needed for that." Whitney signed the relevant paperwork and rushed off in the general direction of her car.

Shona, intent on the crime scene, felt a prickling in the back of her neck and turned around. A small crowd had gathered, thankfully behind the barrier of the crime scene tape. Why the good citizens of Dundee were being so well behaved she didn't know. She spotted a telephoto lens and stomped in its direction.

"Take even one picture of this scene and I'll slap you in the clink."

"You can't arr—"

"Just watch me. There's no way that's making its way to any newspaper, anywhere in the world."

"But—"

"Anywhere." Shona's voice remained low but colder than the ambient temperature.

Adanna Okifor, a local reporter, leapt in. "I agree. That sight's not fit for human consumption." Her usual ebullient demeanour appeared somewhat dampened and her signature grin, missing. She shoved her colleague's giant lens to one side.

"Oi. Cool it. This cost a fortune," but the photographer turned away unscrewing the lens as he did so.

Momentarily, Shona was too shocked to speak. Used to butting heads with the press, she was unsure where to go with this turn of events. Okafor's agreement that is, not the photographer's admonishment.

"Can we work together, to make this more palatable to the public?" The reporter stopped, her eyes glazing over. "I'm not sure dead Christmas icons are the best news coverage at this time of year."

"You do have a heart then?" Shona recovered some of her tattered equilibrium.

"Not only a heart, but three kids."

Shona stared at the reporter, who looked about twelve, then came to a decision. "Meet me at my office later today and we'll put something together." Her eyes narrowed. "Just keep the graphic pictures out."

"One hundred percent." The reporter turned and headed towards her colleague who was taking pictures of the crowd and the woods.

Shona turned to Peter and said, "Keep the situation under control and tell the gawkers to do one. I'm off to brief the boss and speak to our witness again. He might have remembered something."

"Good luck with that one, Ma'am." He grinned at her and added, "Speaking to the boss I mean. The witness will be a dawdle compared to that."

"Pray your best Catholic prayers for me."

Peter, nodded. "I'm already on it."

She and Douglas hurried towards the appropriate tent to

shed protective clothing before heading to their respective cars - Shona to turn the heat up full blast. Sometimes, she thought wistfully about the relative balmy South of England, where she spent most of her life. "Och, I'd miss all the excitement if I moved back," she announced to a nearby robin. The robin seemed somewhat underwhelmed by her proclamation. He flew off.

Jumping into her brand spanking new electric car, she switched on the engine and pointed the nose in the direction of the main road. She was toasty before she passed Camperdown park.

5

In the distance a figure watched their every move. Unobtrusive, in twitcher's garb, standing beside a hide, binoculars in front of its eyes. Ostensibly, watching the birds, instead it watched the police. Watched them darting here and there like so many frenetic magpies or, so the figure supposed, seagulls. Dressed in white, swooping down on every assumed clue, clutching it in triumph and sweeping it off to their nest. The scene brought exquisite pleasure to the watcher, knowing they had been instrumental in this. Knowing a plan was finally coming to fruition. A plan many years in the brewing. The world would sit up and watch as the curse was released. A curse which everyone would eventually know, would save the world.

A hint of a smile played around the twitcher's mouth. Thoughts turned from the scene before them to what was to come. The hint grew in stature allowing a full-blown smile then maniacal laughter. The world, like every Christmas, waited. This Christmas, they did not know for what? Yet.

6

A s Shona approached the blue and grey gulags, otherwise known as Bell Street Police Station, her thoughts turned to murder. Not the murders she'd just seen but wondering if it had possibly happened to the Chief Inspector. The thought of facing him with yet more dead homicide victims was possibly not the best use of her time. She just knew, it would not end well. Working on the 'it's best just to rip it off straight away', strategy, she headed straight to his office. No passing go, no brewing coffee. The Chief was fully in harness and waiting for her. He'd obviously been briefed about the latest homicides, on his arrival.

"Dead Father Christmases. You've surpassed yourself, McKenzie."

"Yes, Sir." Shona knew this was the only response required until, like the latest storm, he blew himself out.

"We didn't have any of these shenanigans until you turned up."

Same old, same old, thought Shona. *You'd think he'd be bored with that train of thought by now. I am, for certain sure.*

"No, Sir."

"Until you turned up, it was mundane things like crossbow shootings, now it's serial killers."

Shona dialled up her levels of bravery and risked an answer. "We're not sure it's a serial killer, Sir." *Not yet anyway. I'm as sure as the chief is, that it will be a serial killer by teatime.*

"Get it sorted. I've already had ex-councillor George Brown on the phone."

"Of course, you have. Sir. I wouldn't expect anything less of the good councillor." Her tone mild, she added, "Are the victims perhaps family members or colleagues of Councillor Brown?"

The chief's eyes narrowed as he said, voice clipped, "How should I know? He didn't say so."

"At a guess, Sir, I'd say it's a high possibility. Dundee is quite a small place." *That and the fact his friends and relatives are usually all over my cases like a rash.* "Have you heard from the Alexeyevs yet?"

"Why would I be hearing from a couple of Russian business-men? Or one I suppose as the other is currently at Her Majesty's pleasure."

"I'm sure Her Majesty is delighted to be hosting him. Is that all, Sir?"

"Yes. Get out of my office and get this solved." His eyes contained more than a hint of, I know you're taking the mick, but I can't prove it. Yet.

"Thank you, Sir." She thought about dressing him up as the Easter Bunny and hoping their latest killer would take a pop at him.

Dumping an extra measure of coffee in the pot, she added water and switched it on. Industrial strength caffeine would be needed if she was to get through this case or even this day. Seriously, how did all those morning DJ's do it, starting their day at 4 am every single freaking day of the year. She looked like a zombie on one indescribably early morning. Sometimes she hated her job. She considered adding yet another scoop of coffee to the pot then rammed the scoop back in the caddy. Some members of her team were bouncy enough without being wired into the bargain. The occasional battle had been known to erupt between Roy and Soldier Boy; too much caffeine would probably act like blue touchpaper. She didn't have time for rutting stags at dawn, or any other time of day for that matter.

Returning to her office she pressed the power button on her computer and was online in seconds. State of the art iMacs and iPhones meant the police were never more than seconds away from paying homage to Google. Or their own databases and search engines. Taking a sip of her coffee, she shuffled herself into a comfortable position in her, equally state of the art, leather chair and started a search. A somewhat surreal one, on dead Father Christmases, something she never dreamed she would ever be doing in the line of duty.

Peace reigned as the search progressed, the coffee level got lower, and Shona's eyes grew wider. "You have got to be joking. Seriously."

She bit back a scream as a deep woof rattled the walls of her office. She swivelled in her chair and came nose to nose with a giant bundle of fur and energy - a Weimaraner dog.

"Fagin, what the dickens are you doing here?"

A large tongue washed her nose in response to the question.

"I guess Jock must be here if you are."

Jock was affectionately known as Auld Jock around the highways and byways of Dundee. A diehard tramp, he strongly resisted any attempts to get him off the streets. Until Fagin came along. The dog wasn't keen on any extremes of weather, so Jock moved indoors and had, so far, stayed put. She stood up and went to find the mutt's owner. Fagin followed.

Instead, she banged into a frazzled desk sergeant. "There he is? Should have known he'd have headed for you, Ma'am. Thought you were still out of office though."

It was a close thing whether Fagin loved Jock or Shona more, as she'd been his guardian for a few days as a puppy. The station had given the rascally pup to him after his old dog crossed the rainbow bridge to doggie heaven. An accomplished thief from an early age, the dog was named appropriately.

"Where's Jock? Are you feeding him up?" Everyone at the station loved the old codger and made sure he was treated like royalty.

"Jock's on his way to Ninewells. The ambulance crew dropped Fagin off with us en route."

"What? What's wrong with him?" Then reality set in. "What are we going to do with a dog? We've enough on our plate."

"Looks like he's fractured his femur. Nasty by all accounts. Needs an operation." Then a grin replaced the concern. "And it's what are *you* going to do with a dog? According to Jock, you're on Fagin fostering duties for the foreseeable." He handed Shona a lead and ambled off.

"Sergeant, take this mutt with you. I can't babysit—"

"Sorry, Ma'am. The boss says no." Back ramrod straight he disappeared around a corner, effectively ending the discussion. There was no arguing with a back like that.

"What the freak am I going to do with you?"

Fagin curled up in a ball and started snoring. There was no discussing the matter with him either.

7

Waking the sleeping animal up, she dragged him to her office, where he promptly nodded off again. How did he ever get so lazy, thought Shona? She decided to take him for a run at lunchtime. It would do her good as well. Then she remembered lunch might not be in her future as she'd a couple of dead Santas on her hands. She'd also need to buy a dog bed and some food for the hound. *By the size of him he must have a healthy appetite.*

God help me. Can things get any worse?

Their witness was tucked up nice and cosy in an interview room, clutching a cup of tea in both hands. He seemed to have stopped trembling. He'd also managed to acquire a copy of *The Courier*. Sometimes Shona wondered if they were running a branch of Dundee Social Services. Working on the fact that any witness should be considered a part of the crime until proven otherwise, Shona intended to question him again. Also, she'd nothing else to go on just yet. There was a 'house to house' in her future but not until the team reconvened.

Wiry and small, never-the-less, the witness must be strong if he spent his days digging graves. Especially, in this weather. The ground would be frozen solid. This got her to wondering if they used motorised equipment these days or if it was all still done by hand.

Dragging her thoughts back to the murders, she switched on the recording equipment and said, "I'd like to go through your statement again if you don't mind, Archie."

"I've no' got anything else tae say. I'm no' lying."

"Of course not. I wouldn't even hint otherwise." She watched the witness's shoulders slump, his breath ragged, and continued, her tone low. "I may be able to help jog your memory."

Line by painstaking line, the statement was checked and verified. He'd left his house at 6 a.m. to get a head start on the days digging.

"I'm a little puzzled by this." Shona managed to shove incredulity aside and keep her voice neutral. "Talk me through how you can dig a grave in the dark?" This being Scotland daylight didn't usually make an appearance until roughly 8 a.m., so a fair question.

"It would take me a wee while to walk through the woods to the cemetery."

"Can I just clarify, why you were up so early, if you were hoping to drive to work?"

"I would have started my dig long oors ago if the car had worked." He glared at her; his teeth gritted. "You asked about digging graves in the dark. I could dig a grave in my sleep after thirty years at it. Also, we've portable lights or we'd never get the graves ready in winter."

Shona shivered at the thought. "I'm impressed by your dedication."

"Are you taking the mick?" Archie's brown eyes had narrowed to slits, giving him a sly appearance. He sat up straighter, no longer shaking.

Shona, deciding she would look into Archie's background, said, "No, I'm being deadly serious." A hastily bitten lip stifled a giggle at the thought of what had just come out of her mouth. The thought of the Chief's face as he uttered the word, "Inappropriate," had her moving swiftly on. "Can you picture what your walk was like. Sounds, smells, sights, anything?"

Archie clutched his mug tighter and closed his eyes. Shona waited patiently, or rather waited whilst she tried not to tap her foot. She took a few deep breaths.

"Nah. Nothing, Hen." He stopped, closed his eyes again and then said, "Mind you, I thought yon headless bodies looked a wee bit familiar."

Shona leaned forward and rested her arms on the desk. "In what way?"

"I'm sure I've seen them someplace."

"Where?"

"Its' hard tae say. I'll have to think."

"You sit there and order your best thoughts on the case. I'll arrange another cup of tea for you."

"Four sugars."

Shona shuddered, switched of the recording, and headed in the direction of a stray copper.

The sugar rush obviously fired up the old man's brain as he provided her with a glimmer of hope. "I'm no' certain but I think they might belong to the Christmas display at Debenhams."

"What. How come you know that?"

"Took my daughters' weans there last night. Late opening."

"Archie, you are a top man. Sit there and enjoy your tea and someone will come and take you home.

"I can walk, Hen. It's no' far."

Shona knew it must be about eight miles but admired the

old man's tenacity. "I insist. Heated comfort all the way. One of our finest vehicles. No expense spared."

Shona grabbed a passing rookie and asked him to make sure her witness was returned to his home in style.

"I'll take him in my Merc, Ma'am." Whistling, he trotted off.

Shona watched him, open mouthed, then frowned. How could a young copper afford a Merc? *Mental note – investigate.* As if she didn't have enough on her plate without worrying about the spending habits of the young and foolish.

8

S hona pressed the disconnect button on the phone just as the door flew open and Roy stumbled through the gap.

"We're back."

"So I see. Is there a reason for the dramatic entrance? Is Jason up in A&E by any chance?"

"No, Ma'am, the accident-prone wee wuss is still in harness."

"Wonders never cease. I thought for a minute we were one man down."

"Nah. We've a full complement of men." He paused and added, "Women on the other hand—"

"What? What's happened? Who?"

"Nina fell over her Manhole Beatnick shoes. Her ankle's the size of a melon."

"Manolo Blahnik. Are the rest of you here?"

"Abigail drove her up there. I think they're going to wave warrant cards and get seen ASAP."

"For heaven's sake." Shona's brow furrowed. Not that she wasn't sympathetic but with a case like this time was of the essence and missing detectives could make or break a case.

"Don't worry. She, and a packet of paracetamol, will be back in the salt mines before you know it."

"Get everyone else to the briefing room. And start praying Nina hasn't broken her ankle" The droopiness in her voice matched the droopiness in her heart. *How in the blue blazes have I ended up in the middle of another cavernous hole of craziness? Even I'm beginning to think I'm the grim reaper.*

Jason trotted off, whistling a jaunty tune; he not being the accident-prone copper for once, had added a certain frisson to his day.

The team were clutching mugs as they clattered into chairs. Not that Shona blamed them or minded. They looked like they'd lost sixpence and found thruppence as her granny said. Or would say it if she wasn't currently in Lhasa on some sort of Tibetan handicraft trip. Shona wasn't sure if she was buying, or making, them but either way her granny's social life was better than hers. And it didn't involve dead bodies. Or sprained ankles.

The fully present and correct male members of her team clutched at the hot mugs as if someone was about to steal them. Considering they'd been tramping around in near zero temperatures, they deserved a spot of liquid warmth, thought Shona.

"What did you find? Anything useful?"

Peter took a huge gulp of builder's brew, swallowed, and said, "Not much in the way of evidence. Footsteps, paw marks, tire tracks in the car park but all minimal."

"Probably legitimate punters out walking their beloved pets. Put out a call for anyone in the area, Roy."

"Usual social media posts, I'm on it."

"I'm meeting with Adanna Okifor later, I'll get it in the press."

Synchronised jaw dropping ensued. Peter recovered his equilibrium first. "I thought you said, you were meeting wi' the press, Ma'am." He paused and then added a tentative, "Is that no' a wee bit unusual?"

"I did and it is. I've decided we need to work with them on this. Spurious headlines are the last thing we need."

Jason gave a low whistle. "You never cease to amaze and surprise, Ma'am. Who'd have thought you'd suddenly be BFFs with a reporter?"

"Keeps you on your toes."

The door opened and Abigail bounced in, followed by a much less bouncy, limping Nina. She was sporting a pair of Balenciaga sports shoes. Shona assumed they were already in her wardrobe, as there was no way she was buying those off the shelf in Dundee.

"The warrior returns. What's the verdict, Nina? Am I one woman down?"

"Not at all, Ma'am. Sprained ankle. The cure is exercise and flat shoes for the foreseeable." It was debatable which was the flatter, tone or shoes. Nina was a high fashion, high heels sort of girl.

"That'll teach you." Roy's grin took the sting from the words.

Nina sank into a chair and said, "You pair can wait on me hand and fist." She waved a hand in the general direction of Roy and Jason.

"As if. You've to exercise remember."

Nina groaned.

"Much as I love the general bonhomie and good will, we've a case to solve." Shona glanced around. "Peter and Roy. Jason and Abigail. Pair up and go house to house. You can take Fagin with you."

"Is Jock here?" asked Abigail. "How is he doing?"

"No, just the wee thief he calls a dog. Jock's not doing so well." She explained about the old man's incarceration in Ninewells.

"We can't take a dog for a stroll while we're working," said Jason. "The boss would give us hell."

"The boss is ordering you to take him. He's got a police ID from when he was here at the beginning of his life, so he's officially on duty. Snap to it."

Grumbling, the others stood up. Shona shouted, "Jason, fetch the mutt from my office. His lead is in the top drawer of my desk."

Jason saluted and loped off after the others.

"I take it I'm staying here and doing paperwork?" asked Nina.

"Nope, you're coming with me to Debenhams. We're off to visit Santa's Grotto."

"This job's a laugh a minute."

"It most certainly is. Never let it be said, I don't show you the high life. Just so you know how high a life it is, we're off to Pets at Home after that."

"Be still my beating heart."

Tay FM provided the only sound in the car until Shona said. "How come you can afford all that designer gear on your pay?

"Some are knock offs brought back from my loving family on trips abroad?"

"Isn't that illegal?"

"I wouldn't know." Nina's tone was neutral.

Shona decided to let it go.

"The shoes are real. Paid for by all the overtime you have us working."

Shona thought for a minute and said, "How would a copper afford a Mercedes?

"The aforementioned overtime. You're keeping us all in the lap of luxury."

"I'm surprised I'm still in a job."

9

"Is there an operational reason we're off to Debenham's Grotto or are you just revisiting your lost youth?"

"Ha, flaming Ha. You should be Alfa stand-up." Shona slammed on her brakes as another driver pulled out in front of her car. She took a couple of deep breaths. "Can no one drive these days?"

Nina, thinking that was a bit pot, kettle, black, decided discretion was most definitely the better part of valour. "The Santas? Debenhams?"

"According to our one and only witness, our dead bodies bear a startling resemblance to the Santa family currently filling up grotto space at that esteemed department store."

"And you couldn't phone them?" Pain made the usually obliging Nina, somewhat on the testy side.

"No. Suck it up. You need the exercise. Plus, it's only down the road. We could have walked the whole way and I've driven you, so stop moaning."

.   .   .

Santa's grotto was all cheery music and garish flashing lights. Shona wondered if Alice, soon to be her stepdaughter, was still young enough for Santa. The mere thought of having to stand in a long queue here, gave her a migraine. Despite the fanfare there was a sign in front of the grotto saying Santa had gone to feed his reindeer. Shona was certain this was a euphemism for feed his face or have a sly fag. She went to the nearest pay point and flashed her ID.

"Detective Inspector Shona McKenzie, I need a word with your Mr and Mrs Claus."

A well arched eyebrow gave Shona the idea the elegant woman behind the till wasn't impressed with her line of questioning.

"We have nothing to do with that monstrosity."

"Then please find someone who has."

"Customer service will be able to help you."

Shona's fragile politeness snapped. "I'm in the middle of a murder investigation with no time to wander around a department store. There are three of you here and not a customer in sight, so can one of you find me someone sensible to talk to."

Scowling, the woman dispatched a young man in the direction of a manager. Within five minutes Shona and Nina were in the staff room clutching coffee and waiting for the Clauses to return. They'd nipped out to a school, where they had a side gig, and were due back any minute.

Shona tapped her fingers on the mug, whilst Nina examined her ankle to see if it had miraculously healed in the last hour. They were interrupted by the return of a brace of Christmas symbols – the elusive Santas.

Shona stood up, showed her badge and extended her hand. A look of horror flitted across Mrs Claus's face before she smiled.

"Jessie Carey and this is my husband, Jerrie."

That won't be confusing at all, thought Shona. I wonder what their kids are called. She dragged her wandering thoughts back in line and ordered them to stay focussed. Jessie and Jerrie did bear more than a passing similarity to the pair in Templeton Woods. However, as they were all dressed in the exact same outfit, this could be mere coincidence.

"We would like to ask you a few questions, if you don't mind." She took in the look of fear and said, "You haven't done anything wrong."

A look of relief replaced that of fear. Shona hoped that it wasn't false relief. A tickling in her gut told her the pair in front of her might be in for a shock.

"My questions may be a little unusual, but they are important."

Nods told her she was good to go.

"Are your hair," she turned her eyes to Jerrie, "And your beard, natural?"

"What? Eh? What a stupid question."

Shona, thinking the same, ploughed on.

"It's important or I wouldn't be asking."

"Yes. I've spent years making sure it's authentic."

"Do many seasonal workers do that?"

"Some."

Jeez, this was like pulling teeth. "Do you know any who do?" Shona crossed her arms and her eyes narrowed.

Jessie, leaning forward, butted in. "We've to get back to work. There'll be a queue of hyperactive weans waiting to see Santa."

"Your elf can entertain them until you get back." Shona rubbed the back of her neck. "Now, these seasonal Santas. And their beards."

In about five minutes they had five names. Three that did

the gig alone and one pair. Given the information they'd just been handed, Shona suspected they'd found the identities of their butchered clauses.

Shona pointed the nose of her car towards Ninewells Hospital – they were starting with the duo. She pulled into an electric charging space and having plugged her car in, they were soon heading in the direction of the main foyer where the hospital had decided to run a Christmas Grotto. It was raising funds for the children's ward. As she suspected, the grotto was closed, with a sign saying Santa and his missus had to fly to the North Pole but they'd be back soon.

"HR it is." Shona set of at a brisk pace.

"Who'd have thought it. Two pairs of twins. Two weddings. Two sets of Santas. You couldn't make it up." Nina struggled to keep up with Shona's fast pace.

"We should write a book."

"I've barely time to read a book, never mind write one. Since you turned up it's been nose to the grindstone." A smile in her voice took the sting from Nina's words.

"Does you good. Plus, the extra money keeps you in style." Shona hid a small pang of guilt well. Her team did wo'k extraordinarily long hours. They had shedloads of overtime barely a minute to spend any of it. Serial killers kept them all on their toes.

A wave of an ID card and the lovely receptionist pointed them in the right direction. They were soon chatting to a young man, who took one look at Nina and fell over himself to be helpful.

The missing Santas were called Jenny and Johnny Carey and they hadn't turned up to work that day. "Not answering any of their phones?" he said not averting his gaze from Nina.

"Have you got pictures of them?" she asked.

Shona was happy to leave her sergeant to it. They might as well use every advantage they could get.

The young man rifled through a filing cabinet and pulled out a couple of green cardboard files. One look at the photos inside and Shona knew they'd identified their victims. Thanking him, Shona and Nina headed back to Debenhams. She had bad news to impart, and this was not going to be an easy conversation.

To take her mind off it she said, "Nina, I think you've made a conquest there. He couldn't take his eyes off you."

"Couldn't take his eyes off my twin peaks you mean." She laughed. Used to the effect she had on men, she merely shrugged it off. "Anyway, I'm spoken for."

"Is Bartholomew, the English surgeon still on the go?" Shona quite liked him and was in awe of his large bank balance.

"Nah. My latest squeeze is, Juan. A Spanish dancer. He's got a huge pair of—"

"Nina, that's quite enough."

"Castanets. I was going to say castanets."

"I very much doubt it. Remember we're friends."

Not only was Ninewells deficient two Santas but now, so were Debenhams. The shock being, not surprisingly, too much for Jessie and Jerrie, they'd gone home to gather their equilibrium and change into less jolly apparel. Shona had arranged to meet them at the morgue later, where they would identify the bodies. She'd leave it to the technicians to work out just how that would happen without revealing the fact the heads were no longer attached to the bodies. Much as Shona loved her job there were aspects of it, she found far too depressing.

They returned to silence; the team were still out canvassing. Shona rang Peter to ask if any help was needed. Apparently not as they were getting through the streets faster than Mo Farah in the 5000m dash. Nary a sole at home. This led to the dreary fact they'd be out again that night. The ring of a phone interrupted this gloomy chain of thought, "DI McKenzie."

"Could you come to reception, Ma'am? There's someone says they want to see you."

"Who?"

"Oh, you'll find out." The desk sergeant hung up leaving her staring at the phone.

Used to this sort of behaviour from nearly everyone in her orbit, Shona took it in her stride, stood up and hurried in the direction of reception, her interest piqued.

On arrival, she did a double take. The Alexeyev twins stood in front of her. Considering Gregor was currently banged up for the rest of his life, this was some feat.

"Who's he?" She pointed at one of the figures hoping she'd got the right one. The Alexeyev twins were identical in every way, so it was a difficult call. Not that there should be twins here at all. "I thought the chuckle brothers had been ceremoniously broken up by the long arm of the law."

"You show no respect."

"Absolutely right. Who's your doppelgänger?"

"I do not know this word."

"Your new twin?" Shona had forgotten the Russian was big on muscle and deficient in the brain department. Although, he did seem to muster up the brain power in to run a highly successful criminal organisation and weasel out of every charge laid against him.

"This is Igor Alexeyev. My brother. He has joined my business."

"Just when you thought it was safe to go into the water, along comes another shark." Shona could swear the man standing in front of her was Gregor. She made a mental note to check he was still under lock and key. Nothing would surprise her when it came to this family of Russian thugs.

"To what do I owe the pleasure?"

"We need to speak with you. On an important matter."

"Feel free. I'm here and waiting."

"In private."

"I'm not in the mood for a cosy wee chat. You may have noticed we are not BFF's"

"You do not talk sense."

Igor said nothing letting his brother do all the talking. He, on the other hand, did all the evil glaring. Shona felt sure he'd had a lot of practice in the brooding expression department.

"And you're taking up my precious time – time which would be better spent arresting crooks, rather than yacking with them."

She heard the desk sergeant laugh and threw him a cease-and-desist type of look. A choking sound informed her he was doing his best to comply.

"We have information which you will find useful."

"For heaven's sake." She turned around. "Come with me."

She marched along to an empty interview room and steered them in. Then she sought out Nina. Omitting to inform her of the sudden emergence of another Alexeyev, she waited for the response.

"Good glory to God, where did he appear from?"

"Sgt Chakrabarti let me introduce Igor Alexeyev. Apparently, he's another member of the Brady Bunch."

"What did we do to deserve this?"

"We will not be interviewed by woman. Get man, now." Apparently, Igor did speak English.

Shona was not surprised that his best phrases were insults. She leaned in close and said, "Listen here, son. You asked to speak to me. One more rude word out of your mouth and I'll find a crime to charge you with and sling your bahookie in jail so fast it'll be there before your crown jewels."

His face turned red, and he opened his mouth. Before he could utter one word, Stephan said, "We believe someone is targeting our business." His tone took the word clipped to a whole new level.

If Shona's jaw dropped any further, she could have cleaned her shoes with her tongue.

She mustered up a coherent thought. "You're expecting me to protect your business? One more crooked than Lombard Street."

"I do not know of what you talk."

"Crookedest street in the world. I'm saying you're not exactly legit in your business practices yourself."

"You cannot prove that. You slander us."

"Whatever, I'm bored with this wee chinwag. Why do you think someone's targeting you?"

"Our Ded Moroz are being killed."

"I'd think they'd be dead if they'd been killed. Who's dead?"

"Ded Moroz. Father Frost."

"What...?" The penny dropped and Shona's jaw did another bit of dropping. "You've got the Father Christmas business in Dundee, sewn up?"

"I have the contract to run the grottos yes. Two of our employees are now dead."

"And you know this, how? We've not released it yet."

"That is of no matter." Stephan gave an imperious wave of his hand. Igor did a bit more scowling. "You will find this killer."

"Nina, slap this pair into a cell and keep them there until I say so."

"You cannot do—"

"I can and I will. Stephan Alexeyev and Igor Alexeyev you are under arrest for impeding the police in the course of an investigation..." She carried on with the whole statement and added, "Cooling your jets in a cell might jog your memory as to who told you about your employees' demise."

"We will want our lawyer."

"Of course, you will. Your wish is my command, gentlemen." Her voice held a frisson of cheer. Having a brace of Alexeyevs in her cells always gave an added zing to her day. Then her shoulders slumped – if the usual conventions were observed, they'd not be there for long. *Damn them weaselly slugs that they are.*

When the pair were safely locked up, Nina asked, "Isn't unnecessary arrest against the Criminal Justice Scotland Act."

"It certainly is but, in this instance, I'm quite within my rights."

"You skate near the edge sometimes, Shona."

"If you're telling me off, at least remember to use my proper title." She grinned and added, "Go phone the battle-axe and tell her Bill and Ben need her assistance."

"Righty-ho. The case is barely hours old and already we're having to face McLusky." Nina hobbled off to do Shona's bidding

. . .

Margaret McCluskey, a local lawyer, had a chest you could use as a bookshelf and a demeanour that would make Genghis Kahn look like a Sunday School teacher. She hated Shona with a purple passion - even more than she hated the rest of the population. Although she did seem to worship the lowlifes she represented. Probably because they kept her in great style. She sailed into the station full sails billowing, broadsides and fully ready for battle, with a face liked a slapped kipper.

"Mrs McCluskey, how nice to see you." Shona turned and said over her shoulder, "Follow me."

She'd no sooner guided the sailing ship into dock, alongside her clients, than a uniformed officer hurried up to her. "The Chief Inspector wants to see you."

"Why?" she said in a voice which rose through all the available notes to a treble.

"Ma'am, with all due respect, I like my job. I just do his bidding, no questions asked."

"Good point. Well phrased." She scurried off to meet her doom. An urgent summons to the boss's office never ended well.

Four Weeks Previously

With a smile and a nod, the figure tucked the floral quilt around their mother and kissed the papery skin of her forehead. Waiting until she drifted off and they were sure she was comfortable, with one last glance they headed for the door. The click, as it closed behind them, flicked a switch in their brain. Their thoughts turned sinister. Cold. Calculating. They'd been planning the perfect murder for months now. Researching. Poring through dusty tomes in the library until their fingers turned black. Spider-crawl writing filled a sturdy notebook. A4 and as black as their thoughts.

One question remained unanswered. Not the sort of query one asked of just anyone. It was a question which required expert knowledge of the type that would have a body in maximum security before the first whispered syllable. Where would one find Gu or Jincan in Dundee. An ancient Chinese poison, not a soul would look for it. Yet, there were whispers in the darkest depths of the web, that it could be found. For a price, of course, for anyone willing to pay it. The source had been narrowed down to three possibilities. One stood out.

Behind the duck pond in Camperdown Park lay a derelict twitcher's hut. In an overgrown area, only a select few knew it still existed, even the park employees didn't go near this area anymore. Someone waited there. Someone who did not know he was facing his last night on this earth. Nor did he know just how important a package he carried as he took his final steps into the dark, Scottish night.

Chinese folklore said that Gu's magical powers could transform a human into many different creatures, including a worm. The worms were left to feast on the Gu dealer's corpse, transforming it into a skeleton as they worked their own special form of magic.

"May I ask why the officer I should rely on the most, is hell bent on persecuting the good citizens of Dundee?"

"Sorry, Sir? I'm not following you." Shona rubbed her jaw. This politeness lark made her teeth ache.

"Why are the Alexeyevs in one of my cells? Again." The last word came out in a roar. "Why can't you leave that pair alone?" His brows drew together as he added. "I thought one of them was locked up for good already?"

All pretence of politeness flew out of the window. "Good citizens? They're a pair of thugs."

"According to Ex-Councillor George Brown, they came here of their own volition to ask for help. This resulted in you locking them up." The chief's face turned such a colour that Shona's hand reached for her phone ready to call the medics.

"Although I'm still unsure as to why there are two of them," the chief added.

Of course, thought Shona, Pa Broon, the biggest thug in Dundee, was in league with the Ruskies. He was so tied up with McCluskey they had an unbreakable bond. She still wasn't sure exactly how. She only knew this lot were more incestuous and sinful than Sodom and Gomorrah. She also knew it would only be a matter of time before the ex-councillor was crawling all over her case like the venomous snake that he was.

"It may seem that way, Sir, but let me explain." She clarified the fact there had been another brother waiting in the wings, and then outlined the conversation with the odious pair.

He leaned back in his chair and studied her. Shona waited quietly. Then he leaned forward, steepled his hands and said, "One interview and then let them out. Despite the fact you feel they are thugs…" Shona's mouth opened, and the chief held his hand up, palm out, "… and I may agree with you, they have never been charged. According to the rule of law, they are upstanding immigrants to our country. That will be all."

"Of course, Sir. Thank you."

Shona left the room, too astonished to even think about the chief's demise. That may just be the first time he had ever agreed with her. Deep down she knew, this time, he was right.

"You're still in one piece then?" Nina stopped massaging her ankle as she looked at Shona.

Shona, too thankful to be in one piece didn't have the energy to argue. "Just about. Leave your injuries alone and let's go interview the Brothers Karamazov." A determined spring in her step, she headed off to the interview room. "Fetch the muppets and bring them along to room three," she said over her shoulder.

"You have arrested my clients illegally and I demand you release them immediately." The words came out of the battleship's mouth before Shona had time to close the interview room door.

"Demand away, sunshine, it aint happening. Not till they've answered some questions."

"I—"

Shona banged the desk. "You know from previous experience if you keep your mouth shut, we'll all be away from here much more quickly."

Margaret McCluskey scowled in what she thought was a menacing manner. Shona thought it made her look more like a gargoyle than she normally did. At least she was quiet, which was always a good thing. They started with Gregor. Shona wasn't in the mood for more threatening louring from the dark and stormy Igor, quite yet.

"An easy question. One quick answer and we can all go home for our tea." Shona smiled encouragingly. "Who told you about the dead Santas?"

"You are very rude. No one is rude to us." He leaned over the table.

"I'm sure they're not but I get to be as rude as I like given the circumstances. It's my nick." She leaned forward until she was almost nose to nose with the Russian. "Anyway, I thought I was being quite pleasant. All I did was ask a question. So, the news? Where did it come from?"

"I do not need to tell you this."

Shona had had enough of the pleasant talk. "Yes! You! Do!" She could almost hear the exclamation marks in her tone. "Especially if you want us to protect your business, as you demanded the minute you put your toe through our door."

"I need to speak to my clients." McCluskey turned around and whispered in Gregor's ear. Then she turned back to Shona. "Give us five minutes."

"Oh, for heaven's sake, you've been chatting for hours. Five minutes. No more."

She and Nina stood outside the door and Shona, on the dot of five minutes, shoved it open. "Okay, are you ready to talk?"

"My client will tell you now."

Shona's flabber was well and truly gasted at the words that came out of the Russian's mouth. She thanked him and said he and his brother were free to go. "We'll be keeping a close eye on the Santa business, so you're hopefully safe."

"You do realise we can't do much about their business except catch the killer?" asked Nina as they walked away. "If any more die, they'll be after us and it won't be pretty."

"Yep. We'll worry about that when it happens. In the meantime, I'm hoping the troops are back and ready for action."

The troops were, indeed, back. The ready for action part was debatable as they were all lounging about drinking coffee. Apart from Roy, who for once appeared to be working and drinking coffee. Either that or he was checking his social media.

"You lot can shake your shanks and move it down to the briefing room." She pointed towards the door. "I'd have thought you'd at least be filling in the relevant paperwork."

"Just having a wee break, Ma'am. All that form filling makes a body tired." Peter took a long gulp of his tea. "Plus, we've a thirst bigger than the Law Hill after chapping all those doors."

Shona assumed he meant knocking on doors. After a couple of years in the job she was getting better at translating Scots to English. Nothing in the Oxford police prepared her for Scottish vernacular. "Top up your cups and we'll regroup."

They unfolded themselves ready to move.

"Quick as you please or forget the drinks. We've a case to solve. The case will be colder than the weather by the time you lot get going."

This got them moving quicker than any other threat. At least there weren't any bacon rolls in evidence, thought Shona. *Thankfully. I don't think my waistline could take all this grease for much longer.*

"So, what did the house to house throw up? Have you arrested our murderer? Got any leads?"

"Sorry, Ma'am. Very little, I'm afraid. No' a soul at home."

Abigail Lau chipped in, "The doors that did open, revealed nothing but Christmas decorations."

"In November," said Shona. "A bit early is it not."

"It's never too early for Christmas," said Nina, a glow in her eyes.

"No one's been out and about for days," added Jason Roberts. "Snow's been too thick and the temperature too low for anyone to move far. Dogs have been performing in the back garden rather than taking a long woodland stroll. Never had snow this early before."

"Charming. Still, it's more helpful than you think. Gives us a vague timeline for the deaths. The bodies have possibly been there for at least five days," said Shona. "I'll speak to Mary later when she's had time to have a look and form an opinion."

Shona had Mary, the pathologist, on speed dial she gave her so much work.

"We'll have to go out again tonight. Sorry guys but overtime's a given until we get a lead on this."

She broke the news to them that the Alexeyevs were once more a duo."

"You've got to be kidding, Ma'am"

"If only I were, Roy. Unfortunately, it's as true as the next bit of news I have to —"

Her phone rang, interrupting her great revelation. "DI McKenzie." She hung up and said, "Sorry, I've got to go. Adanna Okifor is waiting for me. Get that paperwork squared away and we'll reconvene in an hour."

Collective groans greeted her orders.

Okifor had regained her usual cheerful demeanour. "Thanks for seeing me, Shona." Her smile lit up her face making her even more stunning. "I'm sure we can put something together that will keep Christmas sacred."

Shona made a valiant attempt to keep her cool. "That deal may be off the table."

The reporter's face dropped. "Why? What's happened? I've kept my side of the bargain."

"*You* might have done, but your mate with the oversized lens, hasn't."

"The photographer?" Adanna's face took on a look of shock. "What's he done."

"He's been blabbing to the Russian Mafia is what he's done." She paused for dramatic effect. "Large amounts of roubles changed hands, if Bill and Ben are to be believed."

"What's Russia got to do with it?" The reporter's look of confusion was real. Following it by a look of frustration, she said, "I'm going to kill him. He's a loathsome piece of crap anyway."

"That's enough with the talk of killing." Shona took a deep breath, considered her words, and decided to give Okifor the whole story.

Adanna stared at Shona an incredulous look in her eyes. "That's grounds for sacking. Do you mind if I tell the editor?"

"Be my guest. I'll be having a few choice words with him myself. The type that involves Mr Telephoto coming down to my nick and answering a few questions."

Having bonded over a mutual loathing of the photographer, they put their heads together and came up with a plan of what would go in *The Courier* the next day. Adanna was delighted she'd have a scoop and Shona was mildly happy that the story would be put over in a delicate manner. It made a change, as rage was her go to response with anything to do with the press.

On the way to the briefing room, she popped in to update

the Chief. He was less than impressed with the photographer and decided to ring the editor himself. Shona thanked him and headed off with one less task on her hands and an almost jaunty skip in her step.

When she announced to the assembled team that all the Santa concessions in, not just Dundee, not just Angus, but the whole of Scotland were now being run by Gregor and Igor, there was stunned silence.

"Are you telling me that every single Scottish Grotto is in the hands o' the Russian Mafia?"

"Yep. That's exactly what I'm saying."

"Surely that can't be legal," said Iain.

"According to the letter of the law, our pair of thugs are fine upstanding citizens who are being persecuted by Police Scotland."

"I think I need tae retire," said Peter.

"Not a chance. You're here until I leave."

"Jesus, Mary and Joseph, I'll die in harness."

"You can be a right drama queen at times, Peter."

"Nah, I'll take my chances here. Nae chance at home," said Peter through guffaws. "The missus would have me working before I had a chance to mutter gold watch."

The laughter was light relief from their grisly task. They still had two victims on their hands and not a clue or a lead to be found. A chilling thought entered Shona's mind. What if the Alexeyevs were in this up to their long, Slavic necks? She hadn't even bothered grilling them about the murders. Maybe their coming here was a bluff. She shoved the thought aside for the moment. The chief would be all over her like a blizzard if she pulled Dumb and Dumber back in.

"I'm off to meet Jessie and Jerrie at the mortuary, so they can identify our victims. While I'm there I'll speak to Mary. See if she's got any idea as to when said victims died."

"Before you go, Ma'am. I've found something out that might be interesting, or might not," said Roy.

"Go for it. I'll take anything right now."

"I thought the candles might have some meaning." He looked at Shona. She nodded and he carried on. "Red is for Victory, passion and, as we know, blood. The number three in spiritual terms means completeness or perfection. Do you think there might be a spiritual aspect to this?"

Shona gazed into the distance, then returning to the room said, "Good catch. Nothing would surprise me. Explore it further."

Roy's ears turned a light shade of pink. Congratulations from the boss weren't usually forthcoming, mainly because he was usually up to his designer clad chest in trouble.

Shona turned to Peter. "Get on to HOLMES and see if there are any other murders that resemble ours. In any way."

"Aye." He stood up to go, groaning and rubbing his knee.

"Nina and Abigail, find out everything you can about a Dennis Goodfellow. He's been selling info to the Ruskies." Taking in the collected gaggle of confused looks she added, "Our Ruskies." Then added for good measure, "The Bobbsie Twins aka Alexeyev 1 and 2."

Abigail, ignoring her latest words asked, "Any relationship to the Goodfellow and Steven in town?"

"I wouldn't have thought so. He's a snake and they're a reputable business."

The pair scuttled off.

"Jason, work out a route to cover Muirhead, Birkhill and all the houses and villages surrounding Templeton Woods, split it into areas and allocate two of the team to each area. We'll use it tonight."

He leapt to his feet and bounded in the direction of his office.

That left Iain. "You're on forensics. Work your magic and get everything off to the lab. We need results pronto."

Shona was left in an empty room.

14

By the sounds of the screams coming from Jessie, it was clear the body lying in the viewing room was her sister. Jerrie turned all colours of pale, so it would appear the dead man was his twin. Shona asked them both the relevant question to which they replied yes. They had their victims' names. Whilst her heart broke for the pair, knowing the identities of the victims gave them something else to work on. She requested they go to the station to answer some questions. These answers would help to establish a timeline and perhaps the identity of their killer.

"We didn't do it. Do you think we did? Are you blaming us?" Jerrie shook as he struggled to articulate the words.

"It's routine," Shona reassured them. "It may help us with the case.

Jerrie nodded, mute once more.

While Mary finished a post-mortem, Shona was deposited in her office with coffee and a couple of custard creams. A rather nice office it was too, with a functional desk and a comfy sofa.

The pathologist felt she needed somewhere to wind down after doing a post-mortem. Shona, with no time to wind down, took the chance to play the crime scene over in her head. Something was niggling her; the exact details eluded her. Inside her head, every minuscule aspect of the scene was examined in detail. She walked along paths. Scrutinized bare branches, tree roots and hummocks poking through the snow. Took in the bodies – colour, skin, edges of the wounds. No inspirational flashes.

This reverie was interrupted by Mary's arrival. What the pathologist lacked in height, she made up for in personality and bonhomie. "How kind of you to come, Shona, I was beginning to miss you."

It being several months since Shona's last case, the pair hadn't bumped into each other.

"You knew it would only be a matter of time, Mary. How are my latest bodies coming along? Any chance you were working on one of them?"

Mary threw her head back and tinkling laughter came out. "You should be a comedian. They only hit the drawers a couple of hours ago. They've not had a chance to thaw. Frozen bodies are not the easiest of subjects."

Shona chewed her lip, then said, "I'm sure you appreciate time is of the essence on this one."

"I'm sure you appreciate time is not currently on my side. Until they are at the correct temperature, I can't do anything. I've logged every single possible fact I can and they, along with every other pertinent fact, will be with you as soon as I am able."

Shona took a slurp of coffee and shoved the last bite of custard cream in her mouth. Simultaneously swallowing and placing her empty cup on the table, she said, "Thanks, Mary. I won't keep you. I know you're always busy at this time of year."

Mary nodded, looking grim. "That car crash from Riverside. Four deaths, two of whom haven't reached their teens."

"Your job is worse than mine and I didn't actually think that was possible."

"Sometimes, I would agree with you." She massaged the bridge of her nose. "I'll be in touch the second I'm done with your pair." She stood up and waved in the direction of the examination room. "Sorry. Duty calls."

Shona returned to the office with a huge bag of fruit. Cakes had always been the order of the day but most of the team were on a health kick. Those that weren't, could buy their own cholesterol raising treats. She was no longer using her hard-earned cash to support the world obesity crisis. Plus, she needed Peter on the shop floor and him having another heart attack, before Christmas had time to wash its face, didn't feature into her plans. Back in the office she was greeted by an exuberant Fagin who leapt up and attempted to lick her face. "Shove off." She gently pushed him away and pointed to the brand-new dog bed. Jock had trained him well and he obeyed immediately and curled up into a ball. Shona's heart melted just a little bit more. She phoned the hospital to find out about Jock, but they wouldn't give her any info.

"Yir telling me you're the police but, for all I know, you could be lying through yir teeth," she was told in a Scottish accent so strong it could butter toast.

Shona had to admit, they had a point. Might have put it a bit more delicately though. She resolved to visit the minute she could grab said minute.

In her absence the team had been hard at work. Or so it would seem from the mountain of paperwork piled up on her desk. She flicked through it, wandered into the main office, dumped the fruit on the nearest desk, and said, "Meet me in the briefing room in five."

"Minutes or hours," asked Roy.

"Everyone's a comedian. You can meet me there in two minutes, that will cool your jets."

"Sharp as," said Roy and stood up. The others followed suit.

They trailed into the briefing room munching on apples, bananas, and peaches. Shona wasn't quite sure how they were managing to munch on the unripe peaches. She could see a visit to the dentist in someone's future.

She threw a couple of whiteboard pens to Nina and opened Roy's paperwork. "This is fascinating, Roy. Enlighten the others."

"Get set, Nina," said Roy. "You'll needs your wits about you."

Nina uncapped a pen and posed dramatically. The drama soon turned serious. Deadly serious.

"Candles have spiritual significance in several ways. To cut to the short version they are said to banish the darkness of evil within each one of us." He stopped his brows drawn together. "I'm not exactly sure how that helps us. Our killer might think Santa is evil." He shrugged his shoulders.

"Maybe it's someone who doesn't want their bairns believing in Santa."

"Jason, much as your input is valued, that's a bit dramatic don't you think," said Shona.

Nina crossed her arms and leaned against the whiteboard as she watched the interaction.

"All due respect, Ma'am, your cases have drama poured over them thicker than the oil of healing."

Everyone sat up a little straighter waiting for the resulting eruption.

Shona merely threw Jason a look that implied something nasty in store for him, and said, "Carry on, Roy." She gritted her teeth and then, contemplating an expensive dentist visit, eased up a little.

"The number three has many meanings in the bible. It's mentioned 467 times. There are twenty-seven books in the New Testament which is three to the power of three. Christ was dead for three days etc." He stopped and looked at the boss for confirmation he was on the right track.

Shona gazed at him for a minute and then nodded. "Carry on."

"Candles also signify mystery, and the red could be for blood, Christmas or even spirituality."

Shona thought it was time to move on, although it was an interesting avenue. "Where are your thoughts going on how it might link to the case?"

Roy's eyes grew wide. This was a first, the boss asking his advice on a case. He glanced at his notes. "I think the Killer is sending us a message. I also believe it has something to do with spirituality."

Shona rubbed her temples. A headache of gargantuan proportions was threatening to take over her entire skull space, shoving her brain into orbit. "Mmm. You may just be right. There's something in those candles other than Christmas cheer. I think our killer is taunting us." She glanced around the room. "Peter, what did you come up with?"

"Much as I'd like to say, I've solved the case, I've nothing. Well, almost nothing. HOLMES came up with one dead Santa in Lincolnshire."

"Did he still have his head attached to his torso?"

"Firmly. And a convicted felon tucked up in jail for ten years."

"Probably a dead end but I'll give them a ring anyway." Her mouth twisted to the side as she thought. "Go grab some proper food. We'll be hitting the streets soon."

"What about my ankle?"

"Your ankle will be hitting the streets along with the rest of you, and us. They told you to exercise it."

Not needing to be told twice, they scattered to the four winds. Nina's limp appeared to be abating.

15

Their fascination with poisons started with their mother, who told them poisons could be found in the most innocuous of places. Well not quite told but warned. "You better no' swallow them seeds, you'll poison yersel'," rang in their ears on an almost daily basis. At first, they thought the old bat was just a shilling short of a full meter. Then they realised that there might be some truth in the matter. Maybe the useless waste of oxygen was on to something. The library provided a rich source of material for researching all things poisonous. The discovery that the university library was open to any Tom, Dick or Hamish with a Dundee library card was ambrosia to a fledgling researcher's soul. "I've started writing a book about it," was the answer to any curious questions. That was usually the end of the matter. No one thought a teen would really be writing a book.

The researcher's curiosity grew further, the more they delved into this. Page after page, notebook after notebook filled with precise handwriting and fascinating facts. Then, the direction of the research took a more sinister turn. As did the researcher's heart.

This was exactly what they had been looking for. The next question was, just when, and how could they begin this new life direction. Everyone needed a hobby, and this was perfection wrapped up in a huge and glorious enigma. A few more taps of the keys. A few more scrolls of the mouse. A click or two followed by a frown. Eyes narrowed as they focussed on the information on the screen. Then, bingo, the magic formula appeared. This was it. This was how they could move their life forward. A glorious future beckoned. Only one more thing was required.

They turned to the phone. Tapped a few numbers and dialled.
"Hello. This is…"

16

"One more word about your blasted ankle and I'll have you on beat cop duties for a month. That should give you exercise enough to effect a cure."

"It's sore." Misery coated every elongated syllable.

Shona's voice softened. "I know but keeping going is helping it." Then she returned to her usual forceful self. "You'll be heaps better tomorrow. Plus, my ears are in pain from listening to you." She slapped her sergeant, and best friend, on the back, then turned down another path.

Their knock, on the dingy front door, was answered by an older woman clutching a wailing baby. "I'm not interested in Jesus, a new path or double glazing." The door started to close.

Shona shoved her foot in it and flashed her ID card. "Detective Inspector Shona McKenzie and my colleague, DS Nina Chakrabarti."

"What has he done now?" The woman's shoulders slumped, and the baby wailed louder. She patted its back and said, "Come in."

Shona had seen neater sitting rooms after a break in. Where the room had been trashed. Toys and children littered every tiny space. "Are you a child minder?" There were rules about how many kids you could look after at one time. This many weans running around, far exceeded them.

The woman's shoulders slumped. "If only. My daughter and her husband died in a car crash three months ago. They left a mountain of debt and eight bairns."

How Shona stopped her eyes growing wide in shock would remain one of life's mysteries. "I'm sorry for your loss, Mrs…?"

"Germaine. Rena Germaine. What's Joshua done now?" She sighed and signalled them to sit down. "Malachi, go and get your brother from upstairs."

A lad, dressed in Spiderman pyjamas, leapt up and trotted off.

"Joshua. You're in bother again. Granny wants you. So do the polis."

Shona was beginning to feel sorry for Joshua, whoever he was. "He's done nothing as far as we know. We're asking you and all your neighbours a few questions. Is there anywhere we can go that's a bit quieter?"

"And leave this lot. I don't think so. They'd burn the house down or something."

Shona gave in to the inevitable. Keeping her voice low she filled Rena in on the recent murders, omitting the fact that seasonal activities might be a bit curtailed by the identity of the victims.

"Did you see or hear anything unusual in the last few days?"

"With this lot I barely even get out of the door."

A clatter of footsteps was followed by a boy of about twelve. His long hair curled over the collar of his football shirt. Through the blonde locks, Shona could just make out two hearing aids.

"I've not done nothing. I never seen nothing either."

Shona could tell from his voice there was more to this than

met the eye. She looked at his grandmother. "Can I ask him some questions?"

Rena nodded and Shona continued. "You're not in trouble, Joshua. May I ask, do you ever go to Templeton Woods?"

He looked at his grandmother who said, "He's not allowed there." She stared at her grandson who looked down and scuffed his slippers on the carpet. She took a deep breath and said, "Tell the truth. You won't be in bother."

He continued to stare at the carpet.

"It's important, Joshua. You might be able to help us." Shona's voice stayed soft.

He gazed at Shona with blue eyes and said, "Sometimes."

"Were you there a few days ago?"

More toe scuffing. Shona wondered how long the carpet would last with this one in the house. "Yes."

"What did you see?"

His eyes grew wider and said, "How did you know?"

"We're the police, we know everything," said Nina.

His eyes grew wider still. "I'm good really. I didn't mean to do anything."

"What did you do?" His grandmother's tone was sharp.

He burst into tears. "I followed the witch."

Shona couldn't be more dumbfounded if she tried. She glanced at Nina who was trying not to laugh. *Seriously! A witch. Could this case possibly get any wilder.*

"Stop telling lies, young man."

Shona could see an early bedtime in Joshua's future. She stepped in. "What was the witch doing?"

"Running along the path." He sniffled and wiped his nose on his sleeve. "Then she got in a car."

"What type of car?"

"A red one."

'Was it snowing?"

"Yes." He started sobbing. "I ju..., ju..., just wanted to see the woods in the snow. Will Santa not come now?"

"Santa's not coming?" Two other kids joined in the general sobbing and wailing.

"I'm going to have to sort this lot out. Sorry, you'll have to go."

Shona and Nina stood up and headed for the door. The minute they were outside, Nina could not contain her laughter anymore.

"Honestly, a witch? Only you, Shona."

"You do realise we'll have to get that poor woman to bring him to the station so we can quiz him some more." She shook her head. "Eight wee ones. I can't imagine it." To be honest she couldn't even imagine caring for the couple she was about to inherit when she got married. This mothering lark might not be all it was cracked up to be. She wondered what she was getting herself into.

17

Shona loaded her new BFF, Fagin, and all his various accoutrements, into the back of her car. To be honest she didn't think it would all fit. She had no clue that dogs needed so much stuff. Shakespeare, her cat, only needed a collar, food, and flea powder. The minute she opened the door to her flat, she realised that the next few weeks were going to be all colours of fun. Shakespeare made it quite clear that the interloper was not welcome. She threw Shona a look that said, 'He'd better be gone by the time I'm finished eating the food that you are just about to serve me'.

"Suck it up, sunshine. He is here for the foreseeable."

Shakespeare's look said, 'you are going to pay for this'. Shona decided to ignore the look. Her feline companion was getting far too uppity.

Once she had both the animals fed, watered, and tucked up for the night, she poured herself a glass of Talisker whiskey. *I'm getting too old for this. Long days and late nights are for the young.* As she sipped Scotland's amber nectar, her thoughts turned to the poor woman grieving the loss of her daughter, whilst caring for eight children aged five months to twelve years. This led to thoughts of her future stepchildren, Rory and Alice. What type of mother would she be? Would she actually be expected to mother them? Should she just take a step back. This train of thought merely gave her a headache. She took a large swig of whisky and forced herself to think of a subject of which she was surer. Her case. This gave her a bigger headache, so having dumped the empty glass in the sink she headed for bed and swift approaching unconsciousness.

She awoke disorientated and in darkness feeling like she was suffocating. There was something heavy lying on her chest, impeding her breathing. She dragged an arm out from under the lump and switched on the bedside lamp. Shakespeare was curled up on her chest and Fagan stretched out beside her. How had her life come to this? She was young and technically single, yet she was at the mercy of a pair of animal mercenaries. She glanced at the clock, which showed the time to be 5:28 am. Too late to go back to sleep. Shoving the pets to one side, she pulled back the duvet and swung her legs around. She staggered to the kitchen and switched on the Tassimo machine, before showering. The steam and hot water, revived her. Stepping out and wrapping a thick towel around her lithe body she hurried to the bedroom. Grabbing clothes, she dressed. In running gear. She fully intended to run before work, knowing, from experience, that exercise might not feature greatly in the coming weeks. She grabbed the pooch's lead and shouted, "Fagin, time for a walk." The dog came hurtling towards her and screeched to a halt at her feet, a smile on his gorgeous face. She rubbed his soft ears, eliciting a small moan of ecstasy. "Come on daft boy, let's get us some exercise."

She assumed Shakespeare was still curled up on her bed, presumably dreaming of catching mice or eating her next gourmet feast.

Putting one foot outside the door of her building, Shona realised this might not be the brightest idea she'd ever had. There was still a sprinkling of snow on the ground and, where it wasn't snow, a deep layer of frost. Fagin sniffed the air and then jumped onto the street dancing around like a demented marionette. Shona placed her steps carefully, keeping her pace slow, knowing that one missed stride would see her in the exact same situation as Nina. Or worse. She wondered about Fagin's safety. Was he insured if he was injured? Then she remembered the wee chancer was on the police payroll as a police dog. His only purpose seemed to be cheering up the station and keeping Jock staying in his accommodation. That was good enough for police Scotland, so he would be treated if anything happened. The crisp, winter air cleared her lungs and brain, giving her time to think. Although, thinking about Santas and witches just gave her a headache. "The freaking Easter Bunny better not be my next victim or I'm going to go voluntarily on the sick." This despite the only sickness being in the head of the killer. Shona, as always, felt in the pink of health.

Another runner swerved and crossed the street before overtaking her. Probably frightened of dogs, thought Shona. Either that or they were convinced she was a nutjob.

On her return to the flat she discovered six missed calls on her mobile phone, all from one number. The station. This did not bode well. Grabbing a coffee and slugging down several ambrosial mouthfuls of the steaming liquid, she reached for the phone. Before she could press one button, urgent banging broke the silence.

"Okay. Okay. Keep your shirt on," she yelled, in the hope she would be heard over the banging. Opening the door, she was faced with Iain, who'd recently moved nearby. Out of his parent's house and in with his girlfriend.

"We've got a shout. Couple of bodies in Backmuir Woods."

Shona groaned and said, "Come with me." Taking him to the kitchen she poured two coffees, shoved one in his hand, and took the other one with her to the bedroom. She reappeared wearing chinos and the thickest jumper she could find. It left her wondering why murders always seem to take place during the coldest months of the year. She was fooling herself. Murderers were no respecter of seasons around here or anywhere else if it came to it. She added a long coat to the ensemble and pronounced herself good to go.

"You can travel with me," she informed her constable.

A look of horror came over Ian's face. "You're fine, Ma'am. I'll make my own way."

"You wouldn't be frightened of a ride in my car now would you, you wee scaredy-cat." Her wide grin took the sting from the words.

"No. No, you're fine. Just need my car to pick the girlfriend up later."

"I thought you lived with her now, hence the move to the Ferry."

"I do, but she needs picking up from work."

"Okay, I believe you." She hurried towards the door as she spoke.

She knocked at her neighbour's door. Despite the early hour Mrs Gordon was fully dressed and ready to tackle the day. Shona broke the news to her that she was currently fostering a dog.

"It wouldn't be Fagin now, would it?"

"It would indeed." Shona explained Jock's predicament and asked her if she would be willing to look after both animals for the day.

"Of course, Lassie." She nodded sagely. "I know you have a new case on your hands, it's all over the front of *The Courier*."

Shona, who'd forgotten about the rag, pledged to stop and

buy a copy the minute she was finished in Backmuir. As if she didn't have enough to do without more shopping.

"If you find a chance to go up and see Jock as well, I'm sure he'd appreciate a friendly face."

Edna Gordon, who had a soft spot for, and a long-lasting friendship with, the old man, readily agreed. "I'll take him some books. He likes thrillers. Do you think they'd let Fagin in to see Jock?"

"Not a chance." Shona smiled. "But I'm sure you'll think of a way seeing as Fagin is, technically, a police dog."

Edna's eyes twinkled. "Right you are, dear. Off you go and solve your murders. Those poor souls need someone on their side."

18

A rriving at the crime scene, Shona nodded to Sergeant Muir, who waved her through. He allowed Shona to think the crime scene was hers. In actuality he controlled what happened. Once fully suited and booted, she headed towards the relevant area. There was a full complement of her team, all of whom awaited her arrival. They stood back so she could get an unrestricted view of the area. The sight stopped her in her tracks. Just when she thought things could not get any worse. Wrong. Seriously, she did not need this at any time of the year, but Christmas took it to a whole new level of sickening. She wondered what she could do if she decided to change careers. She took a few more steps towards the victims, taking everything in. Then, she pulled her gaze back to the bodies displayed in front of her. Heavy emphasis on displayed. Resplendent, in full royal regalia, lay the three kings or three wise men. Shona was never sure. Like her previous victims their heads were no longer attached to their bodies. And, like previously, there were three candles around each detached head. The team stared at her. "Looks like we've got another serial killer on our hands."

She looked at the victims again. "Poor sods, what have they ever done to deserve an end like this?"

"There's another poor sod over there, who found them," said Peter. He nodded in the direction of a woman sitting with her back against a tree, totally oblivious to the fact her perch was packed snow. Her face as white as her surroundings she shook like leaves in a storm.

"Get her into a police car now," said Shona. "Not only is she in shock but I'd bet my granny on the fact she's also hypothermic." She pointed to Abigail. "You take her and make sure you bump the heating right up. There is a rug in my car you can use as well." The last thing she needed was a witness being dragged up to Ninewells in an ambulance.

Abigail gently led the woman off.

"Do we know who she is?"

"Aye. Name's Catriona McBride fae Dundee. She's an extreme marathon runner and practicing for the Olympics."

"Don't they happen in warmer temperatures? I've never heard of a marathon being run in the winter."

"Och, Shona, as you well know, exercise nuts dinnae care about the weather." His eyes bored right through her.

She thought back to her own run this morning, shrugged, and said, "I suppose."

This case was truly making her feel that she was no longer in the right job. All her cases gave her a feeling of sadness, but this dialled it up to truly wretched. Things always seemed worse at this time of year when everyone should be feeling all festive and jolly. There were now several families who wouldn't be having the Christmas they envisaged. The fact these men might have children waiting for them, who had now lost their daddy, brought tears to her eyes. Her frame slumped as she felt the weight of the world on her shoulders.

She scrubbed at her eyes and said, "Spread out. Do a search." The best thing she could do for these men was to find their killers and she wouldn't do that by feeling sorry for herself. She straightened up and then bent over the bodies. In the absence of Iain, she snapped several photos on her official police phone. What similarities and differences were there between this scene and her previous crime scene? There was still something nagging at the back of her mind and she just couldn't place it. She made a mental note to compare the photos with the ones Iain took of the previous day's victims.

Her thoughts trailed off as her traitorous stomach yelled it was hungry and would rather like a spot of breakfast. She told it to do one and shut the heck up. Now, where had that thought trail been going? Damn, she couldn't remember.

"Lord, Shona, we can't leave you alone for a minute." Douglas and Whitney joined her. Douglas's tone was flatter than usual and even Whitney was not her usual vivacious self.

This case was getting to everyone.

"You don't need me to tell you that all three victims can be declared dead. I think I'm surplus to requirements."

"Have either of you ever seen anything like this before?" asked Shona.

"I'm from Perthshire," said Whitney. "The only serial killer we've ever had belonged to you. I'd never come across any of this until I moved to Dundee."

"What she said, minus the Perthshire bit," said Douglas. "You're the one that attracts the weird and wonderful," he added. "I don't mind admitting, this particular case is depressing me though."

"Any advice on where I even start to solve this, would be gratefully received." She held her hands out to the side in a who knows gesture. "So far, I've got Santas, wise men and a witch. Oh, and just in case that wasn't enough, we've got a spiritual aspect as well. Throw in a bit of black magic and that can take us anywhere and everywhere."

"I'd say you've got yourself a case, Detective," said Douglas. "Go forth and detect. I need to get back to work."

"Me too," said Whitney. "I hope I don't see you again too soon."

I wouldn't stake your pension on it." Shona's words were wasted as the whirlwind sped off into the distance.

Shona directed her next steps towards Abigail and Catriona. The girl had recovered some colour and the shaking all but stopped. It turned out that she had, quite literally, fallen over the bodies. Her teeth started chattering again when she spoke about it. Shona opened the car door wide, as it looked highly likely Catriona was going to vomit again.

"I tripped. Then I realised I was lying on top of a dead body." Her voice reached a high-pitched treble Shona was sure was not there ordinarily. "They... they are... they are... Just lying there. No... no... no... heads." She leaned out of the car and followed through on her ability to vomit. This was followed by dry heaves once all stomach contents had run out.

Shona felt a bit queasy herself. From the state of this girl, she was sure that she had nothing to do with these murders. She might be able to run several marathons in the space of a week but the shock, regarding this incident, was genuine. In fact, Shona could see a lot of counselling in the girl's future.

"Abigail, take Catriona to the station, get her something to drink and ask a doctor to take a look at her." She looked at the girl sitting next to her. "We'll need to keep her clothes, so get her to call someone who can bring her some in. I think it might be better if she has a friend or relative with her when we take her statement. Also, get some DNA as we'll need to eliminate her presence on the bodies."

Shona climbed out of the car and left her sergeant to sort everything out, secure in the knowledge the girl would be safe with Abigail.

Shona joined the others in the search. "Anything so far?" she asked Jason.

"The whole things a complete pig's ear. If we step anywhere, we could be destroying evidence."

"I know, it's a tricky one."

"There are a lot of footsteps in the wider area – probably your average Dundee citizen out for a walk," added Nina.

"The difficulty is, we don't know how long the bodies have been here. Might have been buried under snow for at least a couple of weeks," said Shona, her voice containing more than a hint of hopelessness. "Keep at it."

Two hours later, frozen and with no clues as to what was going on, they trailed back to the Gulags. The blue and grey building that was Bell Street Police Station did not inspire confidence in Shona, never mind the good citizens of Dundee. On a dreich Scottish morning it looked even more depressing than usual.

"You have got to be kidding me," she said to the empty kitchen. A coffee machine deader than her case, meant she'd be reduced to the swill they served in the canteen. Slamming the jug on the counter, she took several deep breaths and forced herself to calm down. Compared to the three new residents of the city mortuary, her day wasn't so bad after all. She headed to the troops office and peered beyond the door. Abigail was a lone wolf.

"Where's everyone else?"

"Not back yet."

"Probably stopped off at a baker of some description."

"Yep. Our witness is tucked up in the relative's room, with her mother by her side."

The room, a newly instituted measure, had a grand name for what used to be a storage cupboard. A large one but a cupboard never-the-less. It was still better than an interview room for the vulnerable. "The doctor's on his way to give her the once over."

"Good job. Can you call an electrician and get the coffee machine fixed? Stat. I'm off to brief the chief." She added as she disappeared through the door, "Wish me luck." She knew, without a shadow of a doubt, a healthy dollop of luck would be needed. Alongside a liberal sprinkling of good fortune.

"Inspector, I was hoping you would show up."

Shona's heart sank even further in her chest. Hearing about a shout, from someone other than her, never led to a good outcome.

"The Alexeyevs inform me you are not taking their case seriously."

Shona straightened her shoulders. *Hang on a flaming minute.* "With all due respect, Sir, it's only been a day and we were hard at it until late last night."

"Ex-Lord Provost George Brown has also been on the phone."

"I knew it was only a matter of time. What's Pa Broon complaining about now."

"Your inability to solve a case."

Shona opened her mouth, but the chief held up his hand. This was happening far too regularly for Shona's liking.

"I'm on your side but pull out all the stops on this. There is only so long I can hold the vultures at bay."

Dumbfounded didn't begin to cover it.

The boss, clocking her surprised look, said, "Contrary to your opinion of me, I do support my staff."

"Thank you, Sir. I appreciate it. I will certainly do my best to solve this case as quickly as possible."

"Preferably without the death rate rocketing sky high. You seem to have a body count rivalling that of the Somme." He glared at her and added, "Also, please refer to Ex-Lord Provost Brown by his correct title."

That glimmer of decency didn't last long. She trudged out of the door.

19

The tantalising aroma of freshly brewed coffee assaulted her nostrils, the minute she stepped outside the chief's office. The team, now back in residence, brought mince pies and large cups of piping hot, caffeine loaded, extra strong coffee back to the station. Looked like Abigail had warned them about the lack of caffeine and Shona's mood, encouraging them to take preventative measures. Shona fell on it like a drought deprived nomad. The people, and assorted victuals, migrated to the briefing room. Peter threw down a copy of *the Courier*. Emblazoned across the front was the Headline:

Dundee Rocked by Double Murder

Dundee, the Murder capital of Scotland, plays host to yet another double murder. Police are, once more, seeking a heinous killer after the bodies of a married couple were discovered by a council worker using Templeton Woods as a shortcut.

The man, a gravedigger, used to working with the recently deceased, found himself shocked to the core when he, quite literally, stumbled across the bodies early yesterday morning.

It carried on in this vein for several more paragraphs, not once mentioning the shocking identity of the victims. The photos were of the police in their white coveralls and not one bit of the bodies could be seen. It finished with:

Police are advising the public to avoid the area. If anyone has any information, please contact DI Shona McKenzie of Police Scotland on 07033 999333

"Bit tame for the courier, isn't it?" said Jason.

"I've temporarily managed to tame the beast," Shona replied.

"Temporarily is probably the word for it," added Nina.

"Enough of the newspaper talk, they're the least of my worries. Nina and Abigail, can you go and take a statement from our witness?"

"Do you not want to do it, Ma'am?" asked Abigail.

"You've built up a rapport. You're in charge."

The slamming of the door signalled their retreat. This left the remainder in, what appeared to be, a clueless hiatus.

"It's no' very easy to find evidence in the snow," said Peter.

"I agree," said Iain. "My photos look more like a shoot for a winter calendar than anything resembling a crime scene."

"I noticed something a bit strange," said, Roy. "It looked like someone had burnt the bottom of one of the trees." He stopped, stroking his chin.

After a couple of minutes, Shona said, "The suspense is killing me. Spit it out."

"I'm sure there were traces of candle wax around the burn."

A bomb went off in Shona's head. "That's what was bothering me about our Santa scene. Did anyone else see it there?"

Blank looks gave her the answer.

"Did anyone get samples or photos?"

More blank looks.

"Iain, take yourself off to Backsmuir Woods. Get photos and scrapings into evidence. Then go see what you can find in Templeton Woods."

"On it." He leapt up and hurried towards the door. "Roy, widen your search and see what else you can find out about symbolism. I'm sure our boy's sending us a message.

"It might—"

Shona waved a hand in the direction of Peter, who had spoken the words. "Yes, I know. Could be a woman. Peter and Jason, you're on HOLMES. See if these murders throw up any similar cases."

Shona, ensconced in her office, picked up the phone and dialled the mortuary, in response to a note that the pathologist was looking for her. Mary, not surprisingly, was in the middle of a post-mortem. Shona left a message for her to phone her back, thus continued the game of telephone tag. Sighing, she pressed the end button and dropped the phone back in its cradle. Opening her computer, followed by a browser, she searched religious symbolism. After ten minutes she leant back in her chair. "What a freaking rabbit hole. Who knew there were so many different practices? Or so many so-called religions either." She had a feeling this was all tied up with one of them, but which one?

The ringing phone dragged her away from her continued efforts down the rabbit hole.

Please, God, don't let this be another murder. Fortunately, it was Mary, the bearer of news. Whether it was good or not, Shona wasn't sure."

"Your Santas didn't die from beheading. They were poisoned."

"What with?"

"I don't know."

"How can you not know? Aren't you some sort of world expert on the subject?"

"Not world but certainly the UK. This is something I've never come across before."

"I'm a tad confused. How can you know its poison without knowing what it is?"

A long story of tissue samples and cell changes ensued. Shona's eyes glazed over, science not being her strong point. At the end of the diatribe she said, "Thanks for the update. Keep me posted when you've got a hit on what it is."

"I've fired off a bunch of emails to international colleagues, so we should have an answer before you know it."

"Thanks."

"Any time. I do like a puzzle, and you always provide me with one. I don't know how you do it."

"I'm not sure myself. It would appear to come naturally."

20

News, whether good or bad, took its own sweet time coming. When it did, it only made matters even more confusing.

Gathered in the briefing room they all stared at blown up and enhanced photos from both crime scenes. Iain had done them proud.

What does that mean? Asked Shona. "Peter, you're our Guru when it comes to all things Dundee."

"Never, seen it in my puff?"

"What are you talking about? For heaven's sake speak a language I understand." Shona's fingers tapped a staccato beat.

"I've no clue. It's no' anything to do with Dundee. If it is, it's new."

Silence fell as they gawped at the pictures once more. They could clearly see flakes of wax and a burn mark. Underneath, faintly etched in the bark of the tree, were the letters VFE.

"Maybe it's something to do with environmentalism," suggested Nina.

"Very Free Environment," added Roy.

"Vivian Fu–" Roy had another attempt.

"Roy, that's enough."

"There is rather a lot of action goes on in weird places, Ma'am," said Roy.

Shona ignored him.

"Volatile Force Environmentalism," Jason speculated.

Shona slammed her hand on the table. The noise reverberated around the room and shut them all up. "Enough with the guessing. Roy, redeem yourself and find out what the letters might mean."

A flash of designer elegance heralded his flight from the room.

"I didn't mean..." She shook her head, accepting the inevitable. "How did the interview go, ladies?" asked Shona, her voice calmer.

"Not gone anywhere yet. The doctor sent her up to A&E in an ambulance. I don't think she's got anything to do with our dead bodies."

"I agree. If she's acting, she should be in Hollywood, not working in Tesco." She turned to Nina. "Make a note to interview her later."

Pulling out her phone and tapping open the notes app, Nina said, "Got it."

"Good. Peter, what about HOLMES."

Peter pulled a sheaf of papers from his pocket. "No' much. Couple of beheadings in the dim and distant past. Nothing like this though and no' staged."

"Another copycat?" asked Shona.

"Could be. Although, I'm no' getting that feeling."

"Are you still thinking along religious lines?" asked Abigail.

"I think it's an avenue worth pursuing." Shona chewed on her lip.

"It's the only avenue we're pursuing," said Jason. "We're not exactly following many trails."

"Everyone's a critic. Maybe if you lot did a bit more work and lot less complaining we'd be further forward."

"They had something similar in Devon a while back. Might be worth speaking to them," said Peter.

"We need to dig deeper. Get a request for info on social media but keep it on the down low." She took in the look on Peter's face. "Abigail, you're on that."

"Jason, you're on the witch angle. Get our wee escapologist in with his gran and interview him."

The detective jumped to do her bidding.

"Peter, any witches covens in Dundee."

"Not a clue but I'll do a google search and get on to my informants." He stood, rubbed his chin and added, "No' sure what VFE has to do with witches though."

"I'm not sure what anything has to do with anything," said Shona, her tone morose. "Except, we've another serial killer on our hands."

The team scuttled off to complete the weird and wonderful, leaving Shona to phone Devon. She wasn't holding out any hope as your average killer didn't tend to take the train between gigs.

"How can I help you, Shona," said her equivalent in Devon CID. "It's not often we get a Scot giving us a bell."

"We've a strange case up here." She outlined the relevant points.

"Strange? Crumbs, I'd say it was off the planet zany. How can Devon be of help and assistance. If you need the English involved, you might be better with Berwick on Tweed."

"Apparently only Devon can help. HOLMES says you've had something similar."

"Have we? Can I do a search and get back to you? I've just arrived, so not quite up to speed yet."

"Sure."

She hung up and opened a list of missing persons. She'd no sooner done so than the phone rang. "There's a school on the phone. They seem to be missing three Magus. Apparently, that's the singular form of Magi."

"Never mind the grammar lesson. Put them through." A frisson of hope ran through her veins. It wasn't often fate played into her hands but maybe she might have a Christmas miracle.

Not quite sure why they rang the police rather than the Magi's nearest and dearest, Shona still found herself tapping the boards outside the headmistress office in St Paul's School. Despite the distance between her and her schooldays, she still felt like a naughty schoolgirl. Nina, on the other hand, remained as ebullient as ever. Nothing got the girl down. Especially now she was back to wearing Prada shoes.

"Never thought I'd be back in a school. Certainly not a Catholic one."

"Were you ever in trouble?" asked Shona.

"Good as gold, me. Never a hitch. Bet you were Head of School."

"How did you know."

Nina laughed. "Didn't take Einstein to be honest."

The door opened to reveal a young, blue eyed, designer clad, bombshell. Headmistresses had obviously moved on since her 600-year-old school head hung up her cane, thought Shona. Private school educated Shona, thankfully never received the cane. Her school didn't get the memo about corporal punishment not being quite the thing anymore.

"Come in ladies." They were offered seats and coffee, which they gratefully accepted. One phone call and bone china cups and a coffee pot appeared. St Pauls - the swankiest council run school in the city. Shona hoped the dishware came from the head's pocket and not the education authority's coffers. She shook her head, took a sip of her coffee, and said, "We believe you have three missing persons."

"We most certainly do. They've turned up for every rehearsal so far and now not a sign of them. Today of all days." The woman frowned, which aged her. Maybe not as young as she first appeared.

"What's so special about today?"

"The BBC are here ready to film the school performance of the Nativity."

"So, you're saying there are three of your students missing. Have you told their parents?"

"They're not students playing hookie; these are professional actors."

"But I thought it was a school performance." Nina was obviously having as much trouble keeping up as Shona.

"We have a mix of school and professional actors. Prince Ali insisted on it."

"You need to bring us up to speed or this conversation is going nowhere." Shona took a restorative sip of tea and settled back to hear the whole story.

It turned out Prince Ali, of some kingdom in Africa, was in Dundee doing a PhD at the university. He wanted his children to have an authentic Scottish schooling experience so sent them to St Pauls rather than the Private School. However, he did a lot of interfering and had arranged for his children's performance to be filmed by the BBC. It was he who brought in the professional performers to beef the whole thing up.

"So, why are you contacting us about the missing Magi and not their families?"

"Because no one has a note of their next of kin."

"What kind of half-baked operation are your running here?" The end of Shona's tether had been reached several minutes ago.

"There's no need to be rude. We got them through an agency, and they have no clue where they are. They've disappeared off the face of the earth apparently." She flicked through a diary. "We last saw them four days ago; the agency spoke to them four weeks ago. They have no record of next of kin."

"Shona took out some photos. Are these your missing actors?"

"Could be. I'm not sure. They always had makeup plastered on their faces."

Shona took their names and the name of the agency. She also asked for the name of the esteemed Prince, since he was the one who insisted on them.

"I'm not sure I can do that. What about His Highness's privacy? He won't be happy."

"What about your missing Magi? They might just be tucked up in the mortuary. I think that trumps the Prince's feelings."

The woman hesitated for a moment, a pulse flickering in her eyelid, decided, and pulled a notepad and pen towards her. She divvied up the details without another word.

After swallowing the cold remnants of her tea, Shona stood and shook the headmistress's hand.

"Thank you for your time."

21

"I've never met a prince before." Nina had a mascara wand in her hand as she retouched her makeup ready for the Royal event.

Shona concentrated on driving. Her idea of a good time didn't involve having Pow Wow's with Princes.

They'd arranged to meet His Royal Highness in his rented baronial pile. At least Shona assumed it was rented. Unless Ali had bought a Scottish Castle especially for his visit. Nothing would surprise her. It seemed to be in the middle of nowhere, on the shores of a loch she'd never heard of. How did those kids get to school of a morning? This got her thinking about getting her own kids to school once she'd married her beloved. Maybe she'd made a mistake. She wasn't cut out for the mothering lark. She had enough trouble ensuring a cat got fed, never mind the insatiable demands of a teenager and a seven-year-old.

"Earth to Shona."

She shook her head and said, "What? Eh?"

"Have you ever met a prince before?"

"Of course, I have. Prince Phillip."

Nina shook her head. "How come?"

"Duke of Edinburgh Gold Award."

"Of course, you did. Why am I not surprised?"

"Shona McKenzie, International Woman of Mystery." She swerved to avoid a cyclist. "At least I would be if I wasn't working twenty-four seven."

"And you talk about us moaning."

"Boss's privilege."

Prince Ali's driveway was longer than Shona's street. The doors to his current pile bigger than her whole flat. Even in a country where castles were two a penny, the one towering before them was impressive. Standing on the shores of a loch, it was tourist brochure perfect. Nina whipped out her phone and snapped a few shots.

"Cut it out, David Bailey, we're working." Shona's rebuke lacked force. She felt like snapping some shots herself.

"Who?"

Sometimes Shona felt every minute of her age. "Never mind."

The door creaked open in true spooky castle style. Shona, in the act of showing her ID card, stopped dead in her tracks. If this butler wasn't Lurch from the Adams Family, it was his twin brother. Recovering her equilibrium, she waved her ID and informed Lurch she had an appointment with the prince.

"Please come in, Madam." Lurch had an accent you could pour whisky into. He showed them to a room that looked like it could house the whole of Bell Street Station and still have room for the car park and indicated they should sit.

Shona, convinced the chair was worth more than her next decades wages, remained standing. The door burst open and a couple of kids, around the age of five or thereabouts, hurtled towards them. One was on a bike and the other a scooter. The prince obviously had more children than the ones at St Pauls.

More door crashing and a young woman followed them bellowing, "Come back you pair of vagabonds." The young woman was obviously learning her English from an ancient source, like Methuselah. Who in the name of all that's holy used vagabond in this day and age, wondered Shona?

An imposing African man, wearing a suit, crisply laundered shirt, and tie, wandered in and spoke sternly. "James and Phoebe, that is quite enough." His voice softened. "Do as Afia tells you." His English was impeccable.

The children stopped, dropped the transport on the floor and hurtled towards him. They each threw their arms around his legs. "Sorry, Daddy." English was obviously important around here.

The man ruffled their hair and said, "Go with Afia. She will find you a snack."

The nanny, or whoever she was, wandered off with her entourage.

"I am Prince Ali. Welcome to my home."

"Your High—" Shona was cut off by the entrance of a tea trolley laden with cakes.

"You must avail yourselves of my hospitality. No one will go hungry in my home." He indicated the trolley. "What would you like?"

Thinking it would be churlish to refuse African hospitality, they grabbed a drink and a cake. Shona somewhat impatiently. How was she meant to run an investigation, stopping for a tea break every two minutes? Honestly.

"Your High—"

"Call me Ali."

"Ali, we need to know more about your children's play. Unfortunately, three of the actors are now dead."

His eyebrows drew together. "I wondered why the play had been cancelled. This is not good."

"What's the drama? It's a school play, not Carnegie Hall."

The man sighed heavily. "My teenagers want to be film stars." He shrugged his shoulders. "Like every teenager in the world. This was to be their debut."

All that fuss and bother with filming, so a couple of spoiled brats could be on the telly. Shona wasn't impressed.

Ali took in the look on her face. "You obviously do not have any teenagers."

Shona thought it was time to move on from the pleasantries. "Why did you hire professional actors from that particular agency.?"

"It was the only one I could find. There are not many in Dundee."

Fair point. Chosen from a cast of very little to choose from.

"Did you meet with anyone from the agency?"

"No. That was not necessary. I am a busy man."

"Did you ever meet the actors?"

"No. Why should I?" The man drew himself up. An imposing figure indeed.

"The fact they would have access to your children, one of whom is probably in line for the throne."

"I come from an impoverished country. Why would anyone be interested in harming my children?"

This bloke is either thick or a good actor himself, thought Shona. "You're not exactly impoverished yourself. You never thought they could get kidnapped?"

"Is this going somewhere, Inspector?" The man's tone had dropped several notches on the coolness scale. "My children's safety is none of your concern."

Unless they get kidnapped or killed you blithering idiot. She contented herself with the thought and merely said. "I have five dead bodies on my hands and it's going down any trail I need to take in order to find a killer."

"Five, who else is dead?" The Prince pushed his obviously designer glasses up his nose, his hand holding a visible tremor.

"No one you need bother yourself with. I doubt you're acquainted with the others"

Ali's face lightened slightly but his eyes still looked troubled.

"There's obviously something bothering you. What is it?"

"You really do not need to concern yourself with this."

"I really do if it has anything to do with my case."

He hesitated. Stared straight at her and said, "My son is missing."

"Is there a reason you didn't tell us this straight away?" Shona's patience had long flown out the window and her face ached with politeness.

"He is eighteen. He disappears often. Young men do."

"When did he go missing?"

"Two days ago."

She requested, and got, a photo of the young prince. Losing visiting royalty didn't look good on anyone's watch. "We'll ask patrol cars to keep an eye out for him."

She left, wondering if the young prince's disappearance had anything to do with the victims she currently had on her hands. Unlikely, but no stone unturned and all that.

22

"**A**part from the posh accent, he didn't seem very regal."
"Maybe he's more princely like in his own realm."
Shona thought her friend's hero worship of Royalty was a little
overstated, but she didn't want to dash her illusions too deeply.

"Where to now? Any chance of a cuppa?"

"You've been drinking tea all morning. Get a grip, woman."

"Those dainty cups don't hold more than a mouthful. I'll die
of dehydration."

Shona drove through a MacDonald's and grabbed two
coffees and a couple of burgers. Gourmet it was not but it filled
a hole. She ate as she drove, keeping a close eye out for the blue
light brigade. She didn't want to push camaraderie too far.

The theatrical agency was on the top floor of a tenement on the
Perth Road. It was a dog and pony show, in that there was one
harried man, a phone, computer and an overall dingy
demeanour.

"I've got no work for you, love," he said to Shona. He took in

Nina's entire body, from her crowning glory to her designer shod toes, whistled and said, "*You* on the other hand."

Shona shoved her ID card in his face, "We're the police, love, and we've got plenty to say to you."

"No, need to get fuc—"

"If the next word out of your mouth involves swearing, I'll arrest you."

"What for? No laws about—" He took one look at Shona's face, took a step bac, held his hands up, and said, "It's all good."

"I'll tell you if it's good or not. One more wisecrack out of that huge gob of yours and I'll be all over your business like the vamp in a seedy movie."

"How can I help you, Officer?"

Shona wasn't sure which of the oily git's personas she hated the most, wise man or obsequious. Her hands were itching to charge him with something. Anything. *I need a holiday.*

"Your name would be a good start."

"Davey Jones."

Shona took a deep breath. "Are you having a laugh?"

"No." He had the look of a man who was fed up explaining his name. "My mother was a wit. What can I say?"

"I need to know more about three actors you sent for a shoot at St Paul's School."

"I'm not responsible for their actions. "He leaned back in his chair and added, "Whatever they've done."

"I should jolly well hope not. I am sorry to have to inform you, they're dead."

A couple of blinks as the agent took in the news.

Shona waited.

"I'd nothing to do with that. Anyway, how am I meant to find three more actors?"

"I've just old you three people have met a sticky end and that's all that's worrying you?" Her look could have cracked the polar ice cap. "Seriously. Could you get any more self-centred?"

"I've a living to make. My wife's lifestyle doesn't come cheap."

"Your income and your wife's spending habits are the least of my worries. What can you tell us about...?" she reeled off the names. "John Starling, David Brennan and Kevin Barnes?"

"Good actors. Just starting out but Kevin, at least, will go far."

"I'm not interested in their Hollywood aspirations. Were they married? Friends, relatives, enemies, next of kin? I'm sure you've watched enough movies to get the gist." Shona's voice travelled a couple of notches up the register.

Nina touched her arm. "Ma'am, may I?"

Shona's mouth snapped shut and she indicated towards the agent.

Nina took over, her voice like honey, reeling the man in and setting the scene to get more information than they ever needed. Shona contented herself with making sure the recording was working and jotting down the occasional note. Funnily enough, under Nina's velvety spell, the agent managed to miraculously find next of kin details for all three of the actors. He also reeled out an alibi that involved an exotic dancer who had crossed Shona's radar in a previous case. The pulse at her temple throbbed. The alibi involved a dance de deux and sheets that were nothing to do with music.

"Thanks, for your help. Don't leave the area without our permission."

"You don't think I had anything to do with this do you?"

"We'll be checking out that alibi in minute detail. I hope the fair," she glanced at her notes even though the dancer's name was burned on her brain, "Tatiana remembers the date and time you hired her services." Her gaze bored into him. "If not, we'll be having an explicit conversation with your wife." Make the little worm squirm. Shona's tolerance levels with lying scumbags who cheated on their wives wasn't just zero but in minus figures. Although she didn't really want to speak to his poor sod of a wife. She had enough on her plate being married to Larry Lothario without cops crawling all over her marriage.

The man slumped in his chair. Being charged with murder or his wife finding out about his extramarital love life was Hobson's Choice – one play he didn't want his life to be in the middle of.

"You played a blinder in there, Nina. Well done."

"Are we off to visit Tatiana."

"We certainly are. Who'd have thought Cat's Eyes would be front and centre in our case. Why am I not surprised?"

Nina threw her designer clad self inside Shona's car.

Cat's Eyes was a lap dancing club owned by the Alexeyevs. Tatiana was one of their 'dancers', a euphemism for prostitute Shona was sure.

Cat's Eyes was locked up tighter than an otter's bum, not surprising as it didn't usually get going until about 9pm. Shona decided the boys could have a night out at the firm's expense and chat the girl up. They'd get the information from the exotic dancer somehow. The level of some that would be involved in that how, she didn't want to know. Sometimes ignorance really was bliss.

23

On their return to the Gulags, Shona sent Nina scuttling to chat to uniform. Whilst Prince Ali didn't seem to be too worried about his missing heir, Shona thought it warranted a higher priority. Especially since the body count was rising as quickly as the temperature was falling. Early in the season for snow, the weather didn't seem to have got the memo. Emergency revival coffee in hand, she summoned the rest of the team to the briefing room.

The team had come up with the square root of nothing regarding moving the investigation forward.

"Dundee's no' big on witches' covens. The last one was Grissel Jaffray in 1669 and local legend has it she's tucked up nice and cosy in a grave in The Howf." Peter coughed and slurped his tea. "She'll no be running around Templeton Woods these days."

"Thanks for that insight, Peter." She shrugged. "This case has me feeling like I'm in the middle of a Grimm's Fairy Tale." A pulse pounded in her temple. She rubbed it and added, "If she did turn up it wouldn't surprise me. Why not a ghost as well as everything else?"

"We probably are, knowing you, Ma'am. In the middle of your man Grimm's tale, I mean. With respect of course."

She turned to him as he scored a withering look. "What's the result with Joshua? Anything more insightful?"

"Not been able to interview him yet. Three of the kids are ill, so the gran can't leave the house. His auntie is bringing him in later."

"I'll interview him. Make it much later as we've all got to go out and break devastating news to some next of kin."

She assigned them in pairs, deciding to take Jason with her. He was getting far too cocky, and she wanted to keep an eye on him. That and the fact he was the most accident-prone bobby on the planet. Without high-heeled shoes she mentally added.

"Empathy and compassion by the bucketload but remember we're running a murder investigation. Find out everything you can about friends, acquaintances, low-lifes. You know the score."

With those words of advice ringing in their ears, the team departed to knock on some doors. The hangdog looks told her they did not relish the task.

Relishing wasn't high on her agenda either. This was the worst job she had as a detective. It never got any easier. They rode in silence, both lost in their own private grief and thoughts of what lay ahead of them.

The beautiful stone-built cottage, in a hamlet with a name Shona could neither remember nor pronounce, lay behind a regimented garden. The man who opened the door had a well-trimmed moustache and a military bearing, which explained the garden. A weed probably wouldn't dare take up lodgings there.

She introduced herself and asked if he was Mr Starling.

"*Brigadier* Starling.' His emphasis on his rank was both prominent and revealing. "How may I help you, Inspector?"

"May we come in, Brigadier?"

His eyes narrowed but he opened the door wider. Years of military courtesy kicked in. "Please do."

Inside mimicked the outside in the pristine stakes. It looked ready for an inspection. You can take the man out of the military, but the military stayed steadfastly and proudly inside the man. Or woman.

A diminutive woman rose as the Brigadier said, "The police would like to talk to us, Martha."

Her face paled. "The ruckus about the tree is over. We paid the neighbours."

Shona hurried to reassure her, although she did think the look on her face was a bit OTT for a dust up over a shrub. "This isn't about a tree." She opened her notebook. "We've been given your names as the next of kin of John Starling."

The woman thumped down into her peony patterned armchair. The colours were migraine inducing powerful. Her face, in contrast, had whitened considerably.

The Brigadier said, "I am not sure why." Not a flicker of an eye as he stared straight at her.

"I'm sorry to have to tell you that John was found dead this morning."

The Brigadier's eyes narrowed. Martha started weeping; without a sound. It was eerie.

Shona waited and when not another word was uttered, said, "Can you elaborate. I'm curious as to your surprise at being named as next of kin?"

"We are estranged from our Grandson." The Brigadier's voice curt, his eyes angry, he stood ramrod straight as if to attention.

Shona stole a glance at the woman. She looked cowed. Beaten. She'd take a bet on the fact the man treated his family like he was running a military operation. Might explain the estrangement as the man put it. "Is there a reason he put you as next of kin? One of his parents may have been a better choice."

"We brought him up. His parents were not fit to raise a child." The man's jaw snapped shut after he fired the words out at breakneck speed.

Shona felt as if she should be ducking a bullet. She also thought it thought it a bit strange that the man did all the talking. From what she knew of the military, Officer's wives usually had a large part to play in boosting their husband's careers and considered themselves to wear their husband's rank with pride.

"Sir, if you could give us the details without me dragging them out of you, we might all be able to get back to our lives." Her tone held more than a hint of command and an inner core of steel.

Martha, dragging a modicum of bravery from the ether, said, "Their lifestyle was more than a little eccentric. It involved drugs." Her voice quavered, "And his mother's death."

Shona let this fact hang in the air before saying, "Was that your daughter or daughter-in-law?"

"Daughter. She never did take the boy's father's name." Pulling the lace edged hankie from her pocket she dabbed at her eyes again.

"He was always such a gentle boy." She stared at a spot beyond Shona's shoulder. "John, that is." More dabbing. "His father was a rogue."

Shona hadn't heard that expression outside a Victorian melodrama. Strange family indeed.

"Shut up, Martha."

The woman's mouth closed tight as her husband loomed large.

"My grandson was a poofter We have nothing more to add, so you may as well leave."

I've plenty more to add, so I aint going anywhere. I'm calling the shots and I'm currently topping the command structure. You, on the other hand, are an arrogant bully. These thoughts ran through Shona's brain at warp speed. Using every ounce of restraint she possessed, she merely said, "Not quite yet. I've still got more questions to ask." She turned to Martha, "Would it be possible for you to get us a cup of tea or coffee. We've been investigating your grandson's death since early this morning and haven't had a minute to grab a drink." Lying through her teeth, she still needed the woman out of the room.

Once Martha had obliged, Shona said, "I take it you did not approve of your grandson's lifestyle?"

"We didn't want any faggots in the family."

"Sir, that seems rather uncalled for. I would ask you to watch your tone." She'd had enough of his bigotry to last a lifetime. The man disgusted her. From the corner of her eye, she could see Jason clench his fists. She glanced at him and shook her head slightly.

"This is my house—"

"And this is my investigation. I would ask you remain polite. Now, can you account for your movements for the last few days?"

"You cannot think I had anything to do with this?"

That's exactly what I think you nasty piece of work. I'd love to throw you in the slammer with a bunch of prisoners who haven't had sex in years. The fact she couldn't utter these words out loud depressed her even further. With superhuman effort she kept her tone mild. "We have to cover all bases. Your attitude towards your grandson's sexual orientation would lend itself to warrant further investigation."

The tea appeared alongside some custard creams. They each took a sip of what turned out to be Earl Grey. Jason coughed and Shona forced herself to swallow.

The Brigadier brought out his diary and showed it to her.

"May I take photographs as I will need to follow up?"

"If you must but I will be having words with your superiors."

"Please do. You may have to join a queue though."

"Are you always this rude?' A tic appeared at the side of his eye. "How dare you take that tone with me, young lady."

Shona, ignoring him, pushed his buttons even harder. "Do you know if your grandson had any partners?"

"I know nothing of his sexual proclivities or partners. Deviants to a man."

"I warned you about your language, you revolting man."

Shona saw a smile twitch at the corner of Martha's mouth. The Brigadier rose from his seat.

With that, Shona ended the conversation, and they left the couple and the tea behind. Shona couldn't stomach much more of either.

"Get that woman down to the station without her husband," she informed Jason the minute the door closed. "I'd bet Jock's life on the fact she knows more than she's letting on in front of her husband."

"Duly noted." As he said the words he tripped and landed on his hands and knees. Before Shona had a chance to say a word he leapt up and examined his hands before using them to dust down his trousers.

"Good grief, Soldier Boy. Why did anyone ever trust you with a gun in the Army?" She stared at the pavement. Not a crack or uneven paving stone to be seen. Shaking her head she said, "Looks like you tripped over nothing more than an itsy bitsy daisy. Are you okay?"

"Fine, Just need a wet wipe."

"Seriously, Soldier Boy, I'm still working out whether you're an asset or a liability."

Jason's cackle rang around the quiet countryside and a couple of collared doves took off at warp speed. "Let's hope the asset side comes up trumps."

Shona thought she saw a curtain twitch.

"We've got to get them split up. She knows more than she's letting on." She glared in the general direction of the cottage. "Come up with something."

"Consider it done."

24

Having made it back without further mishap Shona went straight to her office. Before she'd even taken one arm out of her coat the boss appeared at her door. As if by magic. It must be serious if he'd made the trip himself.

"My office. Now." He swivelled on his heels and stomped out.

Shona, removed her other arm from her outer garment, threw it on her chair and followed. The grim look on his face did not bode well.

"I have just had a phone call from a," he glanced at his notes, "Brigadier Starling. He informs me you called him…" More note peering. "Reprehensible."

Shona kept her tone mild, "I can assure you I did not, Sir." She squared her shoulders, took a deep breath, and said, "What I called him was 'a revolting man.'"

The chief's face turned purple. He took a few deep breaths and exhaled slowly before saying, "Why is it you think you can go around saying exactly what you want to decent citizens?"

The calmness in his voice sent a shiver down Shona's spine. Yelling was his usual go to. Maybe she'd gone a bit far this time.

The chief opened his mouth, but she stepped in before he had a chance to utter one syllable. "Sir, if I may explain." She outlined the conversation. "So, I'm not entirely sure he's a particularly decent citizen."

The chief's face dialled down a colour or two, settling on the border between ruby and rose. Another heart attack averted.

Shona stopped and silence fell. Hands steepled the Chief stared at his desk. Shona waited.

After what seemed like hours but was no more than seconds, he spoke. "It seems like you were provoked."

Shona let out a breath she didn't know she was holding. Her relief was short lived.

"This still does not excuse you. You will write to the Brigadier and apologise." The chief took in her sullen face. "And you will make it sound like you mean it. When you have done that, get on with solving this bally case without alienating half of Angus in the process."

"Yes, Sir." Shona managed to choke out. She left wondering if she could lock the Brigadier and the Chief in the basement of the old Winter the Printers Building down at Shore Terrace. Suitably spooky and barely used, their cold, dead bodies wouldn't be found for months.

Jason, in an uncustomary rush of efficiency and energy, had managed to devise a plan to separate Starling and his missus. He had arranged for the Brigadier to go and identify his grandson's body. To prevent them going as a matching pair, he'd cited some hitherto unknown rule that only one person at a time could go.

Shona's eyes narrowed. "Unknown, meaning it doesn't exist?"

Jason's mouth twitched at the corners. "It's not my place to say, Ma'am"

"Probably better. You might incriminate me. Go escort him and keep him there for as long as possible."

He sauntered off, whistling a jaunty tune, then turned back, "I'll take him for a coffee and swap tales of military derring do with him. That should keep him occupied for a while." A quick salute and a wink and he dashed out of the door.

"What's got him in such a good mood." Roy, glanced up from his computer. "You give him the rest of the day off or something?"

"Something like that. How did you get on?"

"Not a thing so far, but I'm not giving up." He didn't even look up from the keyboard.

Once she knew the Brigadier was safely off the premises Shona sought out Peter. "You're with me. We're off to visit a bullied wife."

"In the middle o' a murder investigation?"

"Yep. Trust me, it's relevant."

Once they were in the car, he updated her on his visit to the family of David Brennan. "Wife and four kids and by the looks o' the bruises on every last one of them I'd say he was a bit free with his fists."

"How did the wife take it?"

"Looked relieved more than anything else." He angled himself towards her. "In fact, she sounded quite chirpy when she told her weans that Daddy wasn't coming back."

"How did they react?"

"Not a chirp from them; they're the quietest bairns I've ever met."

Shona dialled Abigail on hands free and asked her to get on to the hospitals. "See if Rhiannon Brennan or her kids have been seen. Ask Roy to check up on her family – anyone there who might be out for revenge?"

"I'll ask him to check out her finances as well. Might've been a hit."

"There's not many hitmen that chop off their victims' heads. It's usually a bit more subtle." She pressed end.

"Aye, well, Ma'am. It's still a lead."

"I suppose. Silence fell as each retreated inside their own thoughts.

25

Martha Starling shied back like a startled mare when she saw who was standing at the door. Face white, apart from the red rings around her eyes, she took another couple of retreating steps and said, "My husband isn't here." The wobble in her voice indicated tears or fear were not far off. Perhaps both.

Shona, unsure whether to go for soothing or bracing struck a chord between them. "I know. We'd like to talk to you." Taking the lack of a closed door as an invite to enter she stepped inside and introduced Peter.

"Is there somewhere we can sit?" By the look of Martha's complexion Shona was sure she wouldn't be standing for long. Another witness heading for Ninewells in an ambulance would have the `Chief at boiling point.

The woman, pulling herself together, ushered them into the sitting room and offered them tea.

"That'd be"

"We're fine thank you. We had a cup just before we left," said

Shona, still traumatised from the Earl Grey. She'd ask for coffee but was terrified it would turn out to be made with Dandelions or something equally horrible. She threw Peter a cease-and-desist look and gestured towards a chair, "Please, sit down, Mrs Starling."

Martha sat as though the chair was a foreign object but managed to drag a modicum of composure from somewhere deep inside.

"How can I help you?" Her voice, now stronger, was as cultured as the string of pearls around her neck.

"I wondered if there was anything else you could tell us about your grandson?"

"My husband told you everything."

Shona noticed the twitch in the woman's eye. Shona stayed silent.

Minutes passed then Martha took a deep breath, pulled her shoulders back and spoke. "My grandson is…" She paused and said, a tremor in her voice, "Was a delightful boy – gentle, compassionate and yet full of life." She took another deep breath before continuing. "My husband hated him and his life-style. So, he left home."

"Did you have contact with him?

Indecision flickered in the woman's eyes. Then, a decision made she said, "Yes. I saw him every week."

"I take it your husband doesn't know?"

No, and I would like it to remain that way." The steel in the woman's tone gave Shona the impression she was stronger than her husband gave her credit for.

"Do you know of anyone who would want to hurt him."

"He could have had multiple enemies, but we kept the conversation civil."

This poor lad, thought Shona, with a grandmother too terri-fied to move beyond superficialities.

"What about your husband?"

"No. He wouldn't." Her lips formed the words; her eyes said she was lying.

Shona looked at Peter who rolled his eyes. Her look said we'll be all over this business like a rash.

"John's partner? Do you have any contact details?" Shona pulled out her phone and opened an app ready to jot it down.

"Yes." She rattled off an address so quickly, Shona was sure she'd visited.

Shona stood up and Martha and Peter followed.

"You've been most helpful, Mrs Starling. Thank you." She handed the woman a card. "This is the name of an organisation who will be able to help you."

Peter settled himself into the car. "What was thon card about?"

"For battered wives. Abuse takes many forms."

Shona started the car and pointed its nose in the direction of Balumbie.

26

They pondered where they should start. This took careful thought and detailed planning – nothing could be left to chance if the plods were to be avoided. Capture was not in their vocabulary. Failure was not an option, not after the years of research and attention to detail. This gave them an advantage; no slow game this but one of meticulous detail and long-term success. And successful they would be.

Then, a thought, as though pronounced from the Queen herself – strike at the heart of the most celebrated Christian festival in the world – Christmas.

They picked up a pen, opened a notebook and began to write. Every element plotted in painstaking detail. In the tiniest of handwriting. Details were important. Details allowed one to allude capture because nothing was left to chance.

27

B alumbie, an upmarket estate on the edge of the city, was quiet. Shona drew up in front of one of the smaller houses; it was still bigger than her flat.

"What's the betting he'll no' be at home."

"I jolly well hope he is. We need a break."

Peter pressed the doorbell and they waited. Within a few minutes a man dressed in what looked like pyjama bottoms and a sweatshirt opened the door. His hair was rumpled.

He's either up incredibly late or goes to bed incredibly early.

"What do you pair want? Can't a body have a minute's peace?"

Shona showing her ID, introduced herself and Peter. "We're sorry to have woken you."

"You never woke me. I'm a writer on a tight deadline, so you'd better make it quick."

"Please can we come in?"

"Do you have to? I know nothing about the neighbours or any of their goings on. The person next door could be a serial killer and I wouldn't know." He took in Shona's quizzical look. "I'm only interested in fictional crime."

His attitude's a bit odd for someone whose partner is missing.

"Yes, we do." Her tone brooked no nonsense. There was no way she would give news like this on the doorstep.

He hesitated and Peter said, "If you let us in, we'll be out o' your hair soon enough."

He opened the door further and they followed him to an exquisitely appointed sitting room.

"Are you the partner of John Starling."

A wary look flittered across his face. "Yes."

"I am sorry to inform you he is dead."

The man paled and his breathing quickened. Then, a haunted look dropped into his eyes, and he turned and vomited on the pristine, cream carpet. "No. No. he can't be." Tears poured down his face.

Shona pulled a packet of tissues from her bag and handed him several. He utilised them with little effect.

She gave him a few minutes for the first effects of the shock to wear off and then said, "I appreciate how difficult this must be for you, but I need to ask you a few questions."

The man shook his head. "Why are the police involved?" His eyes narrowed. "Was it a heart attack?"

"I'm sorry but it looks like the death was suspicious."

"You mean he was murdered?" The man shrank in front of her eyes. "Who'd murder John? He never harmed anyone." The look of pain was replaced by a look of bewilderment and fresh tears were accompanied by sobs.

"We can't confirm that at present as there will need to be a post-mortem and the Procurator Fiscal will decide if the case is suspicious." *Shona McKenzie you should be ashamed of yourself; lying to the recently bereaved is not a good look.* In all fairness she didn't have much choice given protocol.

"Can I get you a drink or something?" asked Peter.

"Brandy. A large one." He pointed to a teak dresser which had crystal glasses and a couple of crystal decanters on the top.

"Peter did the honours. The man swallowed it down in two gulps and gasped.

"When did you last see John?" Shona handed over more tissues and wondered if she had another pack in her bag.

"A week ago. I've a really tight deadline for my next novel and he moved in with his cousin to give me space to finish," he forced out between sobs.

"Have you spoken to him?

"No. We don't tend to speak when I'm in the zone. It works for us."

That explains the lack of concern when the police turned up and knocked on his door.

"I'm sorry but I've got to ask. "Where were you last night?"

A look of surprise swept over his face closely followed by a look of horror. "You can't think I did this?" His voice rose. "He was the love of my life; you can ask anyone. I'd rather kill myself than him." Weeping, he wrapped his arms around his body and rocked back and forward. "What am I going to do without him?"

"Is there anyone we can contact to come and stay with you?" Shona wasn't liking his words or his actions. Grief did strange things to people.

"My… my… s… s… sister."

"Have you got her number."

He picked up his phone, dialled a number, and handed it to Shona.

The sister lived nearby and was there within ten minutes. Once she appeared, Shona and Peter left them to it.

"Sometimes I hate my job."

"Aye, Ma'am, it's the worst part. I'm thinking he's not our murderer."

"Either that or he's a better actor than our dead ones."

They headed for Bell Street.

28

Two things awaited her return. The first was a note from Devon police asking her to ring, so seizing the moment, she grabbed a coffee and dialled. By the end of the conversation, she was no further forward. Their dead Santa was killed because his brother-in-law hated him; he just happened to be wearing a Santa suit at the time. His killer was tucked up in a jail cell having confessed all, pleaded guilty and accepted his sentence without a murmur. Another dead end.

The second involved an interview room and a ten-year-old.

"Am I bein' arrested, Missus."

"Dinnae you be stupid, Joshua," said a middle-aged woman, who appeared fascinated by nothing more than her chipped nail varnish.

Shona, taking in the woman's clothing, thought she really had stepped into an episode of the *Adams Family*; Morticia sat in front of her, or at least her doppelganger did. She was a bit long in the tooth to be sporting the goth look, still, each to their own. Taking in Joshua's tear-filled eyes she stepped in. "Of course not, Joshua. You've not broken the law." She smiled and the youngster tried out at tremulous smile of his own. "Would you like to help me with the recording?"

This time his smile was real. "Aye." He nodded several times his eyes shining.

She showed him what to do and once the recording started, said, "Interview with Joshua…" She glanced at his aunt, "Second name?"

"Patterson." Morticia's boredom was almost catatonia.

Who in the name of all that's holy would put this useless lump in charge of a kid, thought Shona? The lad could be kidnapped from the car she was driving, and she wouldn't even notice. Either that or she'd be too indolent to give chase.

"Interview with Joshua Patterson, who is helping the police with their investigation."

The young boy squared his shoulders and sat up straighter. Maybe she knew more about kids than she thought. She seemed to have got this one figured out. Finishing the intro, she started the interview proper.

"Joshua, thank you for coming in to help us."

"Nae bother, Missus. I'll help you. You can trust me."

"I'm sure I can, a big boy like you." She smiled. "Call me Shona."

His beam grew larger if that were possible.

"So, tell us what happened?"

"I saw a witch."

"Dinnae you tell lies, you wee brat." His aunt was obviously taking more in than her demeanour suggested.

"I'm no'"

Shona turned to the lad's appropriate adult who had retreated into her slump. "Let him talk." Her tone, though polite, invited no other action than compliance.

"Why did you think it was a witch?" she asked.

"Cos she was wearing a witch's cloak, course." Joshua's face told her he thought she was a plot point short of a fairytale.

Shona nodded in what she hoped was an encouraging manner. "That's helpful. Was it definitely a woman?"

The wee lad shrugged. "Musta been. Men dinnae wear cloaks."

"Wizards do, idiot."

Shona threw the woman a withering look. "Can you please stop interrupting.

"Mighta been a wizard." Joshua's eyes shone.

Shona sighed. This was getting her nowhere. "What time of night was it?"

The lad peered at his aunt through narrowed eyes. He seemed to be weighing up the sense in answering correctly.

"You won't be in trouble. I'll make sure of it, said Shona.

"'Bout nine o'clock." He took in Shona's sceptical look and added, "Got one o' them fit watch thingies." He waved his arm around so Shona could confirm.

"What did the witch…" she stalled the aunt's interjection by adding, "…or wizard, look like?"

"Dunno, it was dark."

Good point thought Shona. "Tall? Short? Fat thin."

"Really tall." He bit his lip. "Really, really tall." He pointed at his aunt an added, "Way taller and fatter than her."

His aunt threw him a look that could kill a roach at thirty paces but kept her mouth shut.

Shona thought the aunt looked fairly fit for someone so indolent. There wasn't a pick of fat one her. "You've been really helpful, Joshua. Thank you." She smiled and said, "No more going out at night on your own, young man. It's not safe."

"Aye, Missus," he said, in a tone that announced the exact opposite.

"We done here?"

"Yes, you are free to go."

As the pair were stepping out of the door Shona said, "Could you tell Joshua's gran we may need to speak to him again." She took in the lads wide eyed look and added, "Just to clarify a few things. He's not in trouble."

"Whatever." Morticia wasn't big on conversation but it suited Shona just fine. Sad to see the young lad go, she was glad to see the back of Morticia.

Two minutes later she wished she was back in the interview room, even if Morticia was involved.

29

"There's another dead body been found, Ma'am." Abigail's voice was much too cheery for Shona's liking.

"Dressed as? Still got his or her head?"

"No details, other than one body, male, back end of Camperdown Park."

"If this is a shepherd, or any other nativity icon, I'm hanging up my badge." She sighed. "I've had about as much as I can take."

"Six murders in as many days can make you feel like that."

"Come on. Grab as many of the team as you can, find a couple of blue lighters and we'll speed towards the park."

With blue lights flashing they were there in under ten minutes. Nothing was very far in Dundee, even without the addition of blue lights it wouldn't take long. The Park was sealed off and, as per usual, there were a group of disgruntled dog walkers standing outside, with an even more disgruntled copper keeping them at bay. Flashing her ID card resulted in the tape being removed and the car continuing its speedy journey. The last part of said journey required walking and some local knowledge.

Shona crouched down at the entrance to what looked suspiciously like a crumbling bird hide. The sight inside was not a pretty one despite the body still having its head firmly attached. This body had been there for some time meaning decomposition had started. Whitney was in attendance and, from her crouched position, declared the body well and truly dead.

"I'm getting paid for nothing here," she said. Anyone could declare all our latest victims deceased." She nodded in the direction of the latest body, "Especially this one."

"Protocol." The voice was deep, male, and made Shona's heart beat faster.

"Douglas, nice of you to join us."

Used to her sarcasm, he displayed his dazzling white teeth in a grin and said, "Anything for you." He crouched down beside Shona and Whitney, staring at the body. "Although this one seems to have its head attached," he added, with some measure of surprise in his voice.

"Yep. Two cases by the looks of things."

"You're upping the anti then?"

"Seems so." As she spoke her gaze darted around the small hut taking everything in. She'd sent the rest of the team on a similar quest around the area, along with a couple of bobbies, including Brian Gevers, who leapt at every opportunity to help out. She was sure she could see a CID, or rather MIT as it was now called, gleam in his eyes. Nothing was jumping out as being unusual but once the deceased was photographed, catalogued, and removed she would take a closer look. She wasn't writing this off as two separate cases quite yet. Careers could end on the twist of one wrong assumption. She also wanted to make sure this poor bloke, whoever he was, got the attention he deserved. No one deserved to end up like this.

Standing up she went over to the bobbies and asked, "Who found him."

"Parkie," one muttered through gritted teeth.

"Speak English and we'll all be able to get a move on."

"One of the park keepers. Jack Smith." His sidekick was beginning to look a lot less green and a bucketful more confident.

"Where is he?"

"I'll show you." He turned to the other officer and said, "Stay here."

"On my own?"

"Stop being such a big girl's blouse."

He walked off with Shona, saying, "He's new to the force. Needs to harden up bit."

Shona, for once in her life, kept her own council, and they were soon at the park keeper's cottage. She rapped on the door, and it was opened by a woman who looked to be in her early thirties.

She flashed her warrant and said, "DI Shona McKenzie. Can I speak to Jack Smith?"

"That's me. I take it you're here about thon poor chap in the woods."

Shona, wondering why the woman seemed to be taking this in her stride, didn't have to wait long.

"Used to be a nurse. Gave it up to commune with nature."

Obviously not the talkative type. She'd either get all the facts without asking or it would be like pulling teeth.

"Can you tell me how you found the body?"

"Went up there to check the condition of the hide. Might've been dangerous and was thinking of tearing it down. The smell hit me. Thought an animal had died. Found yon poor sod, came back here, phoned you lot."

"Did you touch anything?"

"No. Just turned tail and phoned."

"Did anything look unusual on the way up. Anything

disturbed." Shona found herself mimicking the woman's speech patterns.

"It's a park. People wander at will disturbing everything."

Good point thought Shona. "I'm going to get one of my DC's to come and take your statement properly. He may be able to jog your memory. Something may come to mind."

"Aye, okay."

Good luck to whoever gets that gig. Pulling teeth from the bear zoo not a hundred yards away would be easier.

A search of the area uncovered nothing more than frozen leaves, discarded cigarette ends, and sweet papers. Not that they expected anything more given the delay between death and discovery. Shona spent a lot of time wondering why there was never a clue to be found at her crime scenes. It wasn't as if the criminals in Dundee were more gifted than the rest of the world, so how did they manage to elude capture for so long? Sighing, she turned tail and headed back to the hide.

Adanna Okafor, sporting an edgy and impatient vibe, stood behind the crime scene tape. "What's it this time."

"None of your business is what it is."

"You know I'll find out anyway."

"Shove off. You'll get an invite to the press briefing." Shona strode past the reporter, hesitated, turned back and said, "Come to my office in one hour." Then she hurried on her way muttering, "She kept her end of the bargain. I'll throw her something." She was only glad Mr Telephoto was nowhere to be seen.

Adanna's grin brightened the wintry gloom.

The body was nowhere in sight which gave her a chance to examine the crime scene more carefully. Before entering she said, "Iain, get as many photos as you can."

'I'm on it." Eye to the viewfinder and finger on the shutter button he was as good as his word. After a few minutes of manipulating and crouching he said, "It's all yours." He stood up, wiped his trousers down and added, "If it's okay with you, Ma'am, I'll head to the station and make a start on getting these uploaded."

"Go for it." Shona took his place in the hide, careful not to disturb any evidence. Not that there appeared to be much. Using a torch, she examined every inch and every surface. It didn't look like there'd been much bleeding; forensics would tell them more. Crushed leaves, rotting wood, the usual things you would expect in an abandoned structure. She moved outside checked every inch of the wood still holding the structure upright. Nothing. Then, some faint letters caught her eye. She peered closer, squinted, and the eureka moment arrived. Carved into the wood three small letters, VFE. Their killer's calling card. This was the same case. She'd known this deep in her bones. Given Iain's disappearance, she snapped a couple of closeups with her mobile, decided they were good enough and sent them through secure email to Iain.

Standing up she walked, one dragging foot after another, to her car. It had been a long day and it looked like it was going to get longer. She longed for a holiday somewhere warm and sunny with not a dead body to be seen.

30

The team, and copious amounts of hot coffee, congregated in the briefing room. She outlined the latest development.

"Looks like he's escalating?" said Abigail.

"I agree." Shona picked up a dry marker pen and wrote on the whiteboard.

One body – Head remains attached. No Christmas clothing. No ritual displays. VFE.

Two Bodies – Heads cut off. Dressed as Santa. Candles arranged in a ritual display. VFE.

Three bodies – Heads cut off. Dressed as the wise men. Candles arranged in a ritual display. VFE.

The always ebullient Nina, looked like her favourite pet had died. "Not good. Especially if the trend continues."

"Roy, I need you looking even deeper into the letters VFE. I think they're the key, so off you go and get digging." She pointed to the door.

"I've tried everything."

"Try harder."

"Can I—"

"Whatever it takes."

Roy leapt up and bounded off like an excited puppy; Shona wondered if he was panting. She'd deal with any fallout later if what he did could be classed as unorthodox. She shrugged. To be honest, she was getting used to it.

"Jason, you're on the internet as well. Find out if there are any cults which have something against Christmas."

"What about the Jehovah's Witnesses?" he asked.

"That lot just ignore it. They're no' big on wiping it out."

"Okay, I get it. It was just a suggestion."

"Wipe the sulk from your face and get on with the task at hand." Shona wasn't in the mood for two-year old tantrums.

He leapt up and headed in the direction of his desk.

"The rest of you, phones, internet, genealogy sites if you have to, find out if there are any links between the three lots of bodies."

As they all started to rise, Peter said, "What I'm no' getting is why today's body didnae have all the rigmarole the others had."

Everyone slapped back into their seats.

"I was thinking the same," said Abigail. "It seemed a bit understated."

"Could be the first kill," said Iain, "And he hadn't quite got into his stride." He looked unsure.

Shona nodded, "I think you're right." She chewed her lip. The team remanded silent, knowing there was more coming. "Our killer either killed this one by accident and got a taste for it, or he or she developed their plan further after the first kill."

"Maybe the whole thing was planned like this all along."

Nina, looked at Shona, and added, "I've a feeling in my water that this is meticulously planned."

"Much as I believe you, we can't take your watery feelings to court." She pointed at the door again saying, "Work. Concrete evidence my friends." She then hollered after them, "Peter, search missing persons, we need an identity for our latest victim."

"Aye," but the sound was low as he hurried off. Even the usually laconic Peter felt the pressure.

Shona took a deep breath and went to brief the Chief.

"Ah, DI McKenzie, I was hoping I'd see you.

Shona's mood sank even further. "How may I help, Sir."

"You can help by solving this case and getting the Alexeyevs off my back."

Shona wasn't quite sure what Tweedledum and Tweedledee had to do with her cases this time. One was so fresh the rumour mill hadn't even picked up a whiff of the story; the Three Wise Men were actors and nothing to do with the Ruskies. "I'm not following, Sir."

"Apparently, they own a talent agency and three of their actors are currently taking up space in our mortuary."

Shona, at a rare loss for words, stared at him before mustering up, "Is there any Dundee pie that obnoxious pair don't have their fingers in?" Who'd have thought Mr Oily himself would be in the employ of the Ruskies. He kept that one quiet.

"Their business interests do seem to be wide reaching." The chief waved at the door and looked down at his desk.

"Sir, we have another dead body." She waited for the explosion.

The chief's head snapped up. Through gritted teeth he said,

"Just the one. You do surprise me. Is it anything to do with your current case?"

"It would seem so, Sir."

"Then stop hounding me and go and find your killer." He stared at her, then added, "And make it quick."

She left wondering if she could arrange the chief and the Alexeyevs' dead bodies and pass them off as part of her case.

31

The first breakthrough, or at least a glimmer of one, came sooner than she thought. Peter hammered on her door making her jump.

"Good grief, Man. You nearly gave me a heart attack."

Peter ignored her drama. "I've a possible ID on oor latest victim."

"Give it to me." Her pulse steadied.

"Seamus McLaren. Been missing for three months. His sister called it in."

"Have you spoken to Uniform?"

"Aye. Nae sign, and the sister's no' been bothering them, so they've put it on the back burner. He's a grown man so can dae what he wants."

"Go and interview the sister. Take Abigail and give Nina's designer clad ankle a rest."

"Aye." He turned tail and went to do her bidding.

. . .

Fresh out of ideas and feeling antsy, she grabbed coffee and headed in the direction the team. Most didn't even look up, so she had her answer from them. Nina on the other hand...

"You've a look of someone with news, so spill." Shona grabbed a chair and plonked herself down.

Nina hesitated. "I'm not sure it's relevant."

"For goodness sake. Spit it out."

"I've been going through their social media..." She took in the look of horror on Shona's face. Before her boss could utter one word she added, "I got a warrant and passwords from the relatives."

Shona let out a breath she didn't know she was holding. "Carry on."

"I went through their social media. Obviously, they're friends with the victims in their own little Christmas grouping but nothing otherwise. Some friends in common but you'd expect that in a place the size of Dundee."

"Biggest village in the world. Everyone knows everyone, yada, yada, yada. What's your point?"

The only thing they seem to have in common is they all attend churches around Dundee and Angus." She lifted a mug and took a deep swallow, followed by a grimace. "What the..."

"You'll find that's my coffee," said Shona.

"That's not coffee, it's rocket fuel."

"Never mind my drinking habits, anything else to enlighten me other than we've to check every church in Dundee."

"Nothing, although, I've obviously not checked out our latest victim."

"Keep going. Text the names of the churches and I'll speak to the ministers." At least it would give her something to do.

The phone calls elicited nothing. As per usual when someone dies, they were all saints and the world loved him. Apart from

David Brennan. Even his minister didn't have a kind word to say. His exact words were, "If you're looking for suspects, try my whole congregation. He'd upset every last one of them at some point. Even I'd considered prison time and eternal damnation would be worth it to get him out of my hair."

"Wouldn't throwing him out be better."

"God would forgive murder quicker than losing a lost soul."

Shona hung up and ferreted around for some paracetamol. This case was giving her a headache. Either that or it was lack of caffeine and sugar. She headed for the canteen to see if they had a cream cake going begging. Sod the health kick, she needed calories.

Peter's return brought a flicker of helpful news. According to Seamus's sister he lived his life skirting on the edges of the law. Been in and out of prison but usually kept her up to date. She just assumed he was back inside and didn't want her to know. "He'll be in the system with a nice wee record o' his fingerprints and DNA."

"Fabulous, get on it and we'll see if we get a match. Scour his records in case anything leaps out at you in terms of revenge."

"Aye, Ma'am, after I've had a wee cuppie. I'm fair parched."

Shona's Dundonian stretched far enough to interpret that he needed a mug of builder's brew to accompany his search.

It wasn't long before he was back treading the boards inside her office.

"Oor Seamus was a low-life thug and a dealer. He's probably upset half the city."

"How come he hadn't come to your attention? I thought you knew everyone?"

"Usually, but this particular bampot belongs to Angus, so all the arrests belonged to that fine county."

"And he managed to wind up dead in ours. Great. Get on to them and see if they've anything that could be called a lead."

Looks like he hung out with a couple of Dundee dealers as well."

"Get them in."

"I'll send Jason and Roy."

"Leave Roy. Send Abigail."

"Ma'am. I dinnae mean any disrespect to women but this lot might get a wee bit violent."

Knowing Peter, the master of the understatement, she worked out the proper version."

"Fine. You go and take Jason and Iain."

"Right you are."

"And bring Soldier Boy back in one piece."

"That's one thing I can't promise. I'm fresh out o' miracles."

Shona, admitting defeat, said, "Just bring him back."

H e'd no sooner left than the phone rang. She picked it up
and said, "DI McKenzie."

A southern accent, as thick as molasses, poured into her ear.
"Captain Hernandez, from the New Orleans Police Department
at your service, Ma'am."

Shona's brain ran all the way up the shocked register and
back down again before she could say, "How may I help you,
Captain?"

"You can start by calling me Matt."

"Shona."

"Now we're almost kin, I'll get to it."

The man's voice washed over Shona like a warm blanket.
She shook herself, forcing her brain to listen."

"Seems you have a little puzzle going on there, Miss Shona.
A puzzle involving dead Christmas icons."

Shona, not keen on giving any details to a stranger on the
phone, no matter how sexy his accent, said, "Something's just
come up. Can you give me ten minutes and I'll ring you back?"

"I'll await your call, Ma'am."

. . .

A visit to the chief and a coffee top-up later, Shona was back at her desk and looking up the number for the New-Orleans Police Department. No way was she trusting the number she'd been given was real.

The Chief had agreed that if everything panned out, she could chat details with their colleagues. "It's all about international relations these days, McKenzie." He stared at her unblinking and then added in a half reluctant voice. "Well done for checking."

Shona trotted off fairly happy that she hadn't been blasted for stupidity."

She picked up the phone, dialled, and listened to some rather pleasant jazz music for a couple of minutes. "May I speak to Captain Matt Hernandez please?"

"If you give me your name, Ma'am."

Shona complied.

"That's a fine accent, Miss Shona. Ya'll enjoy our lovely music while I put you through."

Halfway through a rather fine rendition of *Bourbon Street Parade* she heard a voice at the other end.

"Shona, thanks for getting back. I would have been cautious as well."

The smile in his voice melted Shona. She sat up straighter in a bid to tell her brain she was a professional. *Focus. Plus, you're a happily engaged lady.*

"Caught." She laughed. "So, our dead Christmas icons?"

"Seems you and I are having a similar problem. Or at least I did have the problem last Christmas and then it all died down."

Shona, lost for words, remained silent."

"Are you still there, Ma'am?"

"Yes. Sorry. We're not exactly next to each other are we."

"I think our bird has flown the Southern nest and ended up in your fine city."

"Do you have anything that could help us?"

"Not a lot, if I'm being honest. I'll send what I've got."

"I appreciate the help."

"We 'preciate how damn hard it is for you, Shona. Most frustrating case we've worked. Email me and I'll get it back by return." He rattled off the email address.

"You're a top man, Matt Hernandez."

He laughed and said, "Have a nice day now."

Shona hung up thinking, day, it's almost bedtime here.

The male members of her team returned empty handed. "Nae joy, Ma'am. One's on holiday in Tenerife and the other's currently occupying a bed in Ninewells."

"Can you go up there and interview him?"

"Aye. Tomorrow. He had an operation a couple of hours ago and they won't let us near him."

She saw Jason looking at his Fitbit and said, "Managed to get your steps in today?"

"I was looking at the time, Ma'am. I need to ring my date and tell her it's off."

Shona, looking at her own watch, said, "Jason, Iain, I've a job for you later tonight. Grab Roy. The rest of you are freed from your shackles."

"You mean you're giving us permission to go to a lap dancing club?" Roy sounded like a toddler on his birthday.

"Yes. The fair Tatiana, yet again, features in our investigation. It's funny how the same names crop up every time."

"What time? I quite like my new lass and don't want to ditch her too early."

"Good grief, Jason. Sort it out between you." She pointed at the door. I want you through that in good time in the morning. No excuses."

"You can count on us," said Roy.

"That'll be a first." She left them to it as they gave each other manly back slaps; she hoped all boys together would drum up the goods.

Silence greeted her as she opened the door, Shakespeare was nowhere to be seen. The cat's usual frantic meowing was also missing. She shouted her name with no effect. Fear caught her breathing; something must be wrong. A man walked out of the sitting room door, and she screamed.

"Steady, Shona. It's only me."

"Douglas, you nearly gave me a heart attack."

"I take it you didn't get my text."

Her hear beat slowed and her breathing steadied. "No, I flaming well didn't. My phone's switched off. Where's the mutt?"

He came over and hugged her. The kids are staying over with my mum, so I thought we could have some us time. The mutt is with your next-door neighbour who's fostering for a wee while longer."

"She melted into his arms and was gearing up to say how much she loved him, when the doorbell rang."

"You have got to be kidding."

Douglas stepped back, disappointment clouding his eyes. "The curse of Shona strikes again."

"There has to be someone else in the whole of Police Scotland who can deal with this crap," she said as she strode towards the front door. She yanked it open ready to yell and then her mouth opened in a perfect O of astonishment.

"Mum. What are you doing here?"

"Can't a mother pay a surprise visit?" She peeled off one elegant calf skin glove "Especially one expecting an arms-wide-open welcome from her loving daughter."

"Of course." She gave her mother a hug. "You remember Douglas." They'd visited Oxford a couple of months previously.

Her mother enveloped Douglas in a hug. "Nice to see you again." She gave him a look that said she needed mother daughter time and he was surplus to requirements.

"I will leave you lovely ladies to catch up." He kissed Shona and whispered in her ear, "I'll see you soon." His breath caressed her ear lobe and did peculiar things to her insides. He departed with a cheery wave leaving Shona with a feeling that she'd rather be curled up on the sofa with him than face whatever had brought her mother to Dundee.

"Your father is acting strangely."

"He's always strange. He's the very epitome of the absent-minded professor."

"Don't you think I know that."

Shona was somewhat taken aback by her usually laid-back mother's tone.

"So, what, in particular, is strange about him now?"

Her mother took a deep breath and the floodgates opened. Tears streamed down her face as she forced out between sobs. "I think he's having an affair."

Shona's jaw dropped. She didn't think her father knew the meaning of the word. He barely paid attention to anyone, never mind another woman.

"Dad? Are you sure? What gives you that impression?" Her eyebrows drew together in puzzlement.

Her mother, pulling herself together, outlined the whole sorry tale – late nights, mysterious phone calls, conversations that stopped when she walked into a room. It did sound to Shona a bit like an affair, but she still couldn't see it. Rather than tell her mother that, she encouraged her to have a bath and relax, giving Shona time to slug back a stiff Talisker and think. This was the last thing she needed in the middle of an investigation. Family drama was scarce in her life, so she didn't have much experience to draw upon.

She'd no sooner got the drink in her hand and was about to take a restorative sip when the phone rang. She slammed the glass down hard on the coffee table. Whisky slopped out and spread across the teak top. *Damn. If this is another dead body, with or without its head, I'm dragging it to Perthshire and letting them deal with the bally thing. I've had as much as I can stomach.*

She gathered her best thoughts together and picked up the phone with one hand. The other she employed grabbing tissues to mop up the whisky. "Shona McKenzie."

"That's a wee bit formal is it not, my dear."

"Dad!" This was getting surreal. She tried a tentative, "What's up."

"I seem to have misplaced your mother. You haven't heard from her have you."

"She's here."

"What? Why is she in Scotland. I need her here."

Shona's dander shot up higher than any decent dander should. Exhaustion, failure, and emotion had her on a knife edge. "She's hiding from you. She says you're acting weird and thinks you're having an affair."

"What on earth gave her that impression?"

Either her father had been taking acting lessons or his puzzled tone was real.

"Late nights. Early mornings. Mysterious phone calls. In fact, the whole nine yards."

His laugh nearly burst her eardrum. "I'm arranging a surprise holiday for her for our fortieth anniversary not stepping out with another filly."

"You're going to have to tell her. before your anniversary is celebrated by your divorce."

Her mother wandered in, and Shona shoved the phone into her hand. "Here. Speak to Dad and sort this out." She left them to it and went to bed with her Talisker and her cat.

Shona was just burrowing down for the night when her mother poked her head around the door her expression a mixture of delight, apology, and sheepishness. She wandered to the bed, kissed her daughter's forehead and informed her she'd be staying for a few days before returning to her loving husband.

"He's booked us a forty-day cruise." Her mother's eyes sparkled with excitement. "I've always wanted to go on a cruise."

"I'm thrilled for you, Mother, I really am, but it's been a long day." Shona's eyelids drooped, exhaustion weighting them down.

Her mother gave a cheery salute and left her alone.

Crises over, Shona turned over and fell into a deep sleep. She dreamt of headless bodies chasing santas on a cruise ship and woke up more exhausted than when she'd dropped off.

Shona left a note for her mother and drove to work with the air conditioning on full blast, wondering if she should stop off and buy some matchsticks to keep her eyes open.

She was on time, but every member of her team had miraculously arrived before her, something never previously known.

"Roy, in my office."

She'd no sooner taken off her coat than he appeared clutching a large mug of coffee which he handed to her.

"You're a wise man, Roy MacGregor."

"I rather like my head, Ma'am."

Shona smiled, despite her tiredness. The lad, who used to be the bane of her life, had grown on her. "So, Tatiana? Update."

"We managed to get her on her own away from the Alexeyevs but she knew who we were."

"Don't tell me you got nothing."

"I didn't say that."

"Spit it out; we're taking root here."

"The lovely Tatiana confirmed she was with our talent agent. I won't repeat what she said, just be sure it involved a lot of detail."

"TMI, Roy. TMI." She ran her hands through her hair. "Anything else?"

"Nada. We're clueless in every respect."

"Hop to it and find me something I can use."

He trotted off whistling a cheery tune. Shona put her head in her hands and groaned. Time for paracetamol. She was thinking of taking out shares in the company that produced it given that she was single handedly supporting their profits.

Peter poked his head around the door and informed her he and Abigail were off to visit the dealer up in Ninewells. He'd obviously decided the man had been rendered incapable and harmless by his recent surgery.

"You might want to update them on his career choice and warn them to keep their drugs secure."

A ringing phone interrupted her reverie. "It's Mary. I've got a result on the poison that your killer's using."

"Mary, you're a legend."

"Wait until I tell you what it is. You might not be quite so enamoured of me after that."

Shona groaned. "Why is nothing ever easy."

"Why indeed. Anyway, your victims were poisoned by Jinca."

"You what?" Shona massaged her temples and wondered if there was anything in evidence stronger than paracetamol

"Jinca, or Gu, is an ancient Chinese poison. It's as rare as the proverbial hen's teeth."

"This is Dundee not Beijing." Shona stopped, took a couple of deep breaths, and said, "Where in the name of all that's holy would someone get that in a wee Scottish city?"

"That, my dear, is your problem, I am pleased to say. I diagnose. You solve."

Shona found herself listening to a dead phone. "What a flaming debacle," she said as she hung up.

Peter's return yielded more information and no steps forward.

"According to our dealer, Seamus was a right bampot." He took out his phone and read, "I'm quoting directly here. 'He deals in well dodgy stuff. Naebody else would touch it. Dinnae want to get on the wrang side o' him, you ken.' That's something coming from Willy Dermid, who would kill his granny if it meant money." Peter shut his note app and slid the phone in his pocket.

I thought he was low level dealer?"

"He's obviously escalated. I'm a wee bit out o' touch."

"Given the news I've just heard, I'd lay bets on the fact that he had a deal with our killer which ended in his own death." She rubbed the back of her neck. "I'd say, with no fear of being called a liar, this was our first murder in the case. Grab the team and I'll update everyone."

"Could this case get any stranger?" Nina, on a health kick, took a sip of her ginger tea, and added, "This is weird even by your standards."

"Thanks for that insight. Really helpful." Shona swallowed a large mouthful of her own fully loaded coffee. If anyone wrestled that away from her, they'd find themselves playing the next corpse. "I can't get my head round this case at all. Dead drug dealers, mysterious Chinese poisons, and an attack on Christmas. Nothing matches."

"What do you want us to do, Ma'am?"

"I wish I knew." She gathered her equilibrium, remembered she was a leader, and did her best to lead. "I want Roy on finding the meaning of VFE and the rest of you searching

HOLMES for any deaths whatsoever that mention Jincan or Gu." She paused, then added, her face grim, "No one eats, sleeps or drinks until we find something."

Shona updated the Chief, who looked singularly unimpressed and told her to just get on with solving the case. He also informed her his nerves had been fading fast since she arrived on the team and the last one was fraying at a rapid clip. She returned to her office wondering if she could get hold of a spot of the Chinese poison in order to top the Chief. Sighing, she decided solving the case was a better option than murder. She fired up HOLMES.

I t was time to ramp things up. This next part required greater planning, more careful attention to detail, and a yearning to push the boundaries further than ever; so far it would blow their minds.

They pulled a notebook forward and started to write – slow even strokes, deliberate and pushing the pen into the pages. The pages filled up as the plan formulated and grew larger with every errant thought. Every detail meticulously penned and easy to read. The fact they were the only person who would read this was of no consequence. Once dead, this would be a record of who they were and what they did, so it must be legible with no room for doubt.

Their thoughts flew faster than their fingers as page after page filled with the distinctive penmanship, honed at school, and developed further over the years. Future authors would write books about their exploits, so it was important to ensure these authors had everything they needed. Even in death they wanted to make sure every detail was correct.

Their reverie was halted by a stray thought. Was this too big for immediate action?

Thoughts spiralled and crashed in their head. They turned the page and wrote down two more carefully considered sentences, then sat back and thought some more. Reaching over the notebook was closed with a satisfying thump.

S hona put her computer to sleep and shoved her leather
chair back. She'd had enough of computer searches to last
a lifetime. It was time for some action. She picked up the phone
and asked the Sheriff for a search warrant.

After a few seconds silence, he said, "It's rather widespread
but given your case I'll grant it this time."

Shona expressed effusive thanks and hurried to speak to her
opposite number in Uniform. He agreed she could have extra
officers, so her plan was a go.

Heading to the main office she tightened said plan further.
"We're going to do a search of every outhouse and garage within
a five-mile radius of the dump sites. I, and all the sergeants will
head up a team. Peter, you're in charge of setting areas. We'll be
ready in thirty minutes."

They all leapt up. "Can, we ask why? Asked Nina.

"Are we looking for anything in particular?" Abigail was
reaching for her coat as she spoke, radiating eagerness and efficiency in every move.

"These bodies were killed elsewhere and transported. I think our killer has a lab somewhere." The very thought of it sent shivers down Shona's spine and chilled her blood.

Shona, covering Camperdown Park and a section of Muirhead, had Roy and four uniforms in her team. "Listen up everyone. Roy, you take James and Keira. Blair and Mohammed, you're with me."

They all shuffled around. "Roy, your team is doing the outside of the buildings. My team, inside." She glanced at her phone and added, "Roy, keep your phone on. Satellite pictures will be coming through from the Duty Sergeant."

"Roger that."

"You have seriously got to stop watching American cop shows. Okay. Let's hit the first outbuilding."

They headed towards one of the storehouses. With the park being given the heads-up, Jack Smith was there waiting for them. As she went to open the battered wooden door Shona said, "We'll need the keys and some peace."

Jack, who Shona suspected had been a military nurse given her instant obedience, handed over the keys without a murmur and left them to it.

The door at the ancient brick building opened, with a creak and a lot of scraping. Stepping into the first room, it was apparent from the get-go that this was not their killer's lair. It was packed to the gunnels with paraphernalia and a cockroach would have difficulty getting up to mischief in the space left over. Still, Shona wanted to show due diligence, so she called for Roy and asked him to clear an area all the equipment could be stored in. While he prepared and searched a suitable and fairly dry area, she rang Jack and kept her up to date. Her response, "It's a load of old tat anyway," gave them the required permission to be hauling things out. Not that they needed it but neither did she need complaints from the Council's Park Department. They set to moving and shifting just in case the junk was hiding a secret cave; twenty minutes later they had their answer – nothing. The next room was empty in every sense. A blind man could have told them at fifty paces there was no blood, just piles of straw and old horse manure that hadn't been disturbed for years. The remaining rooms yielded even less.

Shona grabbed her phone and dialled the station. "Can you send a forensic team out to – she rattled off the location. Better to be safe than sorry; missing something would have the boss down on her harder than a Glenshee avalanche. She didn't have troubles to seek as it was.

They moved from building to building, inch by brain freezing inch. Their search ended with nothing more than possible frostbite and, in Shona's case, a trip to the bakers. Comfort food was very definitely needed. As was copious amounts of coffee. She seriously hoped that the others had come up with something. If a break was ever needed it was now.

The others looked slightly less miserable than her and Roy but that wasn't saying much.

"Shona, I've some spare clothes in the car if you feel you need them." Nina's look said it all.

"Shona looked down and took in her mud-streaked clothes. "I've sports gear in my locker. That'll have to do. You lot grab something hot and get these down you. She plonked down four boxes of the baker's finest cream cakes and doughnuts. "I'm off for a shower."

"You might want to wash your hair as well, there's a spider's web draping it. There might even be a spider in residence," said Jason.

Shona shrieked and, to gales of laughter from her colleagues, bolted from the room. She stripped, showered in water so hot it could boil a lobster, washed her hair twice and returned to her team looking like she was about to run in the Olympics. At least she was warm and clean. As Roy was in new attire, she assumed he'd done the same. The only difference was, he was still all designer elegance.

"What did you find? Please tell me you found something."

"We found a couple of luxury cars, recently reported stolen. A couple of upper-class, under the counter car dealers are now in custody."

"Uniform are probably throwing a party as we speak. It doesn't help us much though."

"It doesn't help the car owners either. One Porche and one Tesla have now been detained as evidence."

"My heart bleeds. What about the rest of you?"

"Not a thing. If any of the search areas have been used as killing ground, then I'm retiring." Peter leaned back in his chair and stretched out his legs. "I'm done in. It's back breaking work this."

Shona, catching Jason's look, suspected that the bulk of the work had been done by anyone other than Peter. Still, given he'd had a heart attack not so long ago she was willing to cut him some slack. Also, someone had to keep the younger team members in check. He could hardly do that if he was humping and dumping, and he was probably keeping an eagle eye on every single thing that was going on. If there was anything to be found, Peter would have found it. She'd bet her granny on that.

Her phone rang. Her mother informing her she was off round to Shona's grandmother's and Shona could join them there for her tea.

"You'll be hard pushed. She's in Outer Mongolia, I think. Or could be Chile. I can't keep up."

"Why didn't I know that?"

"Probably because you would have tried to talk her out of it."

"There's no need to be rude, Shona McKenzie. I shall take you out to dinner instead."

Shona, groaning inwardly, agreed outwardly. The last thing she needed at the end of a punishingly long day was dinner with her mother. Still, it would save her having to cook and her mother, much as she loved her, was never famed for her cooking skills. Also, she needed the light relief. She phoned her neighbour, grovelled, and asked if the fostering duties could be extended for another night. Thankfully, the answer was yes. The big lummox of a dog would have her mother off her feet in a second and she'd no time for a relative with a fractured femur.

Two hours, five mugs of coffee, one computer search, and a basketful of mind-numbing paperwork later, Roy burst through her door like the charge of the light brigade.

"I've got something for you."

"Enlighten me using your indoor voice."

"Sorry." His grin said otherwise as he practically hopped from foot to foot.

"For heaven's sake, the suspense is killing me."

"I've pinned down a lecturer at the university who's some sort of guru on all things religions and the various sects spawned by them."

Shona sat up a little bit straighter with a hopeful glint in her eye. Not wanting to get too excited before clarifying every tiny detail, she asked, "And that helps us how?"

"I'll bet you my next pay packet that she'll either know about VFE or can find someone who does."

"So, you're still on the religious angle?"

"Yep." He grinned. "Worth a try."

"Phone her and make me an appointment." She didn't want to drag the poor woman in as she wasn't, strictly speaking, a witness. She shouted at his retreating back, "Her name would be helpful."

"Valerie Dickenson," and with that he disappeared.

Shona arrived at the university within the hour. The receptionist blinked twice, scrutinised her ID card and escorted her through a maze of corridors. Shona knocked on a door bearing the name, Dr, Valerie Dickenson, PhD. Impressive. Surely, she must know her stuff.

"Come in."

Shona entered. "Shona McKenzie, thank you for seeing me." She flashed her ID and then offered a hand which the woman shook.

"If you don't mind me saying, you don't look much like a detective." Her smile took the sting from her words, as did the soft Irish brogue.

Shona laughed. "You make a fair point. Outdoor searches, mud, and posh clothes do not make great bedfellows. Sorry."

"You're grand. How can I help you? Your detective mentioned you were interested in VFE?"

"It's popped up at several crime scenes lately."

"I'm surprised. They're so off the radar I had to search my archives to remind myself what they were. VFE are odd but usually fairly docile, so why the police interest?"

If docile involves killing people and chopping off their heads, then I've grasped the meaning of the word wrongly, thought Shona. "Can you tell me something about them? I'll come on to why once I've heard you out."

"We'll start at the beginning. It stands for Voodoo for Everyone. They—"

"Voodoo? Voodoo? What on earth has voodoo got to do with Dundee?" *Maybe there's more to the New Orleans tip off than meets the eye.* Confusion, chaos, and jumbled thoughts mixed to produce no sense whatsoever. Every step forward in this case brought a greater level of crazy.

"Not a great deal as it happens, hence my surprise. I'll get on to that." She waved her hands around, emphasising her points. "It's an international group which stems from New Orleans. They're a break off group, from a break off, group from a break off group. So, pretty much doing their own thing." She paused and glanced at the notes in front of her. "They worship voodoo queen, Marie Laveau. She—"

"Who in the name of all that's holy is she?"

"Holy doesn't come into it, not unless you consider voodoo holy. Many people do." She turned a page. "Marie's soul parted company with her body in 1881. She was New Orleans born and bred and her tomb is in a cemetery in that city. It's a bit of a shrine these days."

"Did she go around killing people."

"Not at all. She took the city by storm through charm. Wormed her way into every stratum of society apparently."

"So, if she died one-hundred-and-forty years ago in the American voodoo capital, how have her supporters surfaced here?"

"There's a medium sized branch in Scotland, and there was a church," she used her fingers to denote quote marks, "here in Dundee. I'm not sure how active it is right now, but I can make some enquiries."

Shona thought for a moment and then decided to come clean. "This is confidential."

She looked at Valerie, who nodded.

"Sealed lips."

"Have VFE got anything against Christmas?" She outlined what was happening.

Valerie took jaw dropping to a whole new level. She also looked a bit green around the gills. "No. No. There's never been anything like that. Not that I know of…" She tailed off then added. "I write mystery novels and if this was a plot, I'd say it was too far-fetched.

"I wish it was a fiction plot. It would be better than this nightmare."

"I might use it." She took in Shona's face and said, "That was a joke. There's no way I'd use that in a book."

"I need the names of group members."

"That might be tricky. They make the FBI look like they have loose lips."

"I'm sure you'll understand that I need your best game on this."

"I'll do what I can, but I need to give you fair warning, they're a secretive bunch and thumbscrews and torture are illegal these days."

"If you even get a whiff of a name, I need it. Pronto. I'm sure you know lives are at stake and I'm terrified the next victim will be Baby Jesus.

The woman shuddered; her eyes clouded. "No one wants that."

"Precisely. Use everything you've got but leave the interrogation and torture to us."

"I'm sure you're excellent at it. I'll throw in everything I've got." Her eyes brightened again, a piercing blue once more.

They shook hands and Shona left her to it. Shona's heart was marginally lighter as they had at least moved one step closer to closing the case and throwing this vile piece of excrement behind bars.

38

She hot footed it to Peter's desk. He was lounging with a copy of The Courier in his hand. A cup of tea sat in front of him, and the remains of a doughnut lay on his plate. He slapped the paper on the desk when he saw her and wiped his hands on a napkin.

"Wee lunch break. I was famished."

"Never mind that. What do you know about Voodoo for Everyone?"

"Never heard o' them. Why're you asking?"

"Apparently that's what VFE stands for."

"They've never come up in any case I've worked on." He sat up straighter. "Let me see what my mates have to say."

"Serving and retired." She shot back, standing up.

"You're no' asking for much."

"I have every confidence in you. Experienced sergeant like you shouldn't have any problems."

. . .

Next it was Jason and Iain's turn. "I need you out putting leather on concrete. Track down every informant in Dundee and find out if they know of an outfit called Voodoo for Everyone."

"You what?"

"Is that what VFE means?"

The pair spoke at the same time.

"Yep. Gold star to Iain."

"Do you think it's a good thing to be broadcasting this far and wide? Might give our killer the heads up." Iain had that are you half-baked look in his eye. It was a look Shona often experienced.

"I'm in two minds but we've nothing else to go on." She chewed on her lip. "Let's rattle them. If they think we're on to them then the dead bodies might stop piling up."

The pair leapt up, grabbed coats, and headed for the door.

"What's your plan?" She was speaking to the air. She only hoped they'd figure out a plan en route. They'd matured and it might be time to loosen the shackles a bit. She just hoped she didn't live to regret it and crossed her fingers behind her back just to be sure. If she was near a piece of wood she'd have touched that as well.

Abigail had a bit more news for her. "I've figured out a link."

"Hallelujah. Hit me with it."

"Hallelujah is closer than you think. Every last one of the victims were Christians." She stopped to let Shona take this in.

Shona's shoulders slumped. "I knew that. Nina came up with it hours ago.

The normally placid Abigail took the opportunity to turn bristling into an Olympic sport.

"What we didn't know is, this lot are all evangelical Christians." She added for good measure, "They're the lively crowd."

"So, now we've got a dead voodoo queen and a bunch of

evangelicals rubbing shoulders with each other. What in the actual heck is this all about?"

"Voodoo queen?"

Shona updated her and said, "Can you do a search for any crime related to Voodoo, anywhere in the UK?"

"There's never a dull minute in Dundee. The Isle of Sky was a positive backwater compared to this."

"You're telling me. Are Skye looking for a Detective Inspector?"

Nina was as gobsmacked as the rest of the team. Shona set her to on HOLMES to see if anything to do with Voodoo came up. Any freaking glimmer of information at this moment would be gratefully accepted.

Shona occupied herself ringing Cornwall to see if they'd had a sniff of voodoo anywhere around their dead Santa. It was a long shot, but she was ready to try anything. She hung up with a net result of nada and picked up the phone again."

"Howdy, Shona. Have y'all solved your case now." Southern charm dripped from every sexy syllable.

If I wasn't engaged, I'd be looking up flights to N'Orleans. She appraised her new BFF of the situation re Voodoo For Everyone.

"How on God's good earth have they come up in your investigation?"

"Apparently, they've got something against Christmas."

"Lordy, Miss Shona, that's the first I've heard of any such goings on. They're a peaceable bunch; keep themselves to themselves"

Shona scowled and took a deep breath. "Is there any chance you could do a bit of digging? Looks like the Dundee branch has gone off piste. Peaceable is not how I'd describe them."

"Leave it with me, Ma'am, and I'll see what I can do."

"You're a top man, Matt Hernandez."

And sexy as all get out, she thought as she replaced the receiver. *That voice does things to my insides.*

Before she could think one more thought, such as ringing round churches, the phone rang. It was the desk sergeant. "You might want to head towards the interview room, Ma'am, your detectives are back."

"And you're telling me this, why?"

'Needs more than two of them." With that Shona was left listening to a dead line. Situation normal.

She hit end with great force. "Why does everyone in this station feel they can order me around." The furniture was singularly unimpressed by her pronouncement and declined to answer.

39

She could hear the ruckus before she was anywhere near the interview room. Throwing the door open with so much force it nearly shattered the wall. She shouted, "Shut up."

Silence descended and all three occupants swivelled to gaze at her.

"What the freak is going on." She glared at Jason and Iain. "You pair, outside now." They scuttled out the door.

She then turned to the one remaining heavily tattooed occupant and took in the handcuffs. "And you can wipe that smirk off your face and sit down. One more peep out of you and I'm adding disturbing the peace to whatever charges we've already dragged you in here for."

"You can just f—"

She slammed the table. "I said shut up."

She stormed out, pointed at another door and said to the waiting detectives, "In there."

Once they were seated, she asked, "Spill. I asked you to speak to informants, not arrest them." She took in Jason's rapidly swelling eye, "Or brawl with them." Her tone could turn the

Sahara Desert into the Antarctic. She threw Iain the sort of look that said I thought better of you.

"Why is Atilla the Hun in female form cluttering up my interview room?"

The shifty eyed pair looked at each other.

"You…"

No, you…"

"You'll have me swearing in a minute." She looked at Jason's eye again and decided. "Iain, spit it out. I'll probably get more sense from you."

Jason opened his mouth, but Shona cut him off with a waving finger. "Not one word."

Iain shuffled a bit then said, "She was resisting arrest."

"And you were arresting her, why?"

"She's a dealer."

"A dealer. First I've heard of any female dealers in Dundee."

"She's come out of nowhere. Apparently, she's been ruling the roost for several months now."

"I'm still foggy as to why you were arresting her." She gritted her teeth. "When I asked you to find out information."

"Jason, needs to tell you the next bit."

Shona took a deep breath and said, "Soldier Boy?"

"One of my informants hinted that she'd taken over from our dead Gu dealer."

"Hinted! You arrested her on a hint?"

"And the fact she's Seamus's cousin."

"Good grief. Why did I have to wring this from you? You didn't think to bring her in here for a chat rather than arresting her."

"She told us in rather colourful language what we could do to each other and our mothers," said Iain.

"Then swung a fist at the nearest Junkie who—"

"Don't tell me he's dead?"

"Nah, but on his way to Ninewells for an x-ray."

"Good God in heaven, why do I have you lot." She took in Jason's eye. "Are you okay? Do you need an x-ray?"

"Nah, I'm Gucci."

"Go and find some ice. Iain, ask Peter to come in. He can help me interview..." She stopped then added, "What's her name?"

"Clodagh."

The pair disappeared before Shona could utter another word. Shona went to find a strong cup of coffee. She needed to be wired to the gills to deal with this new twist.

"A female drug dealer?" The usually implacable Peter had an incredulous hint to his tone.

"Why not? We're all about equal opportunities these days."

"I'm no' getting why the Dundee menfolk are letting her away with it."

"You've not seen the size of her yet. She'd have the bravest of Dundee lowlifes cowering in their shoes."

"I need to do a few weeks on the beat to catch up."

"It can be arranged. But not until we have our killer behind bars."

The minute they stepped inside the interview room the almighty racket started up again."

"This is false imprisonment. I've no' done nothing, you cannae keep me."

Shona could swear she saw the walls shake. "Shut up." She slammed her fist down on the already battered table. It shook harder than the walls.

Shona switched on the tape, read the usual warnings, and said, "We've got you on two counts of assault, one on a police officer and the other on a passing citizen."

"He's a low-life, scumbag junkie and shouldnae have been there anyhow."

"He's now an injured low-life, scumbag junkie." She added for the tape, to avoid future lawsuits, "Allegedly."

Clodagh leaned forward. "And you're pig scum. I'll no telling you anything." "She glowered at Shona and spoke again. "You're dead."

Shona also leaned in so far, she could almost taste the woman's fetid breath. "Add threatening a police officer to those offences."

She sat up again.

"Peter said, "If you threaten the inspector again, you'll have me to deal wi'"

"I'm no faird o' any fat pig."

Peter tensed, but before he could say another word, Shona said, "That's quite enough." Her voice could crack glass but, fortunately, the only glass in the room was the lightbulbs which thankfully remained intact.

She pulled some paper forward and picked up her pen. Given the video this was more for show. "I've had enough of this tittle tattle. I hear you've taken over your cousin's business."

"I'm no telling you anything. I want my lawyer."

"As you so kindly gave my officers the details before you arrived here. Mr Runcie should be here any minute."

As if rehearsed, there was a knock at the door and Runcie himself was issued in. Angus Runcie, a bigger weasel than Margaret McCluskey, if that were possible, also happened to be the battleship's brother. Shona shuddered to think what their parents must be like to have spawned this pair.

"What is my client being charged with?" He slammed his briefcase on the table.

Shona smiled and said, "It's good to see you too, Angus. Always a pleasure." She ran over the salient points and said, "We also want to have a wee chat with her to see if she can shed light on one of our cases."

"It would seem my client was provoked by your officers. I need to talk to her alone before she answers any questions. I am instructing her to remain silent."

"That's almost a relief given that foul mouth of hers. You can have thirty minutes. That should give you time to concoct a story... I mean get a sufficient brief from your client."

"I will be reporting you to your boss."

"I would expect nothing less. The chief inspector will be delighted to see you."

Shona and Peter headed for the coffee room. "Do you enjoy riling them up, Shona." Peter's eyes crinkled at the corners as he tried to contain a grin.

Shona burst out laughing and he gave up the fight and joined in. "Of course, I do. It's great sport."

"The chief will have you for breakfast."

"I've set a nice chocolate éclair aside for him. That should sweeten him up and take the sting out of his words."

"You're a wise woman, Shona McKenzie."

"It's been said, but not often." She changed tack and a serious tone ensued. "Any headway on your search?"

"Nothing, everyone's as puzzled as us. None of them knew yon lot even existed."

"So, what's made them come out of the woodwork now. Also, what's it got to do with New Orleans."

"Aye, Dundee and New Orleans are no' exactly cosied up to each other."

"There's 4,410 miles between them apparently."
Aren't you clever?"

"I spoke to Professor Google." With that, she drained her coffee, shoved herself off from the countertop and said, "Let's go Interview Clodagh." Then she added, "Actually, put Abigail and Jason on standby. I'll ring the sheriff and get a warrant to search McLintock's address."

Peter, slamming his mug into the sink, said, "Grand idea."

"Meet me in the interview room in five." Shona pulled out her iPhone and dialled.

40

The shrill ring of a mobile phone broke the freezing stillness. Birds, startled from slumber in the branches above, shot into the air squawking their outrage.

The figure stopped, stepped behind a tall pine tree, pulled out a mobile, glared at the number and stabbed at the screen.

"What do you want?"

They listened.

"No way. That's not happening."

Silence once more as they listened to the response.

Their face red, they forced out through gritted teeth. "Fine. Give me twenty-four hours."

They swivelled on the balls of their feet and jogged in the direction they came from, treading carefully to avoid gnarled roots and patches of ice. This was no time for accidents.

They felt for the packet in their pocket and shoved it deeper, then zipped the pocket tight. This was too precious to waste. If in the wrong hands it could eliminate half the population of Dundee. In their hands victims would be methodically selected.

They slipped from the woods and ran along the now paved

street – just one more foolish runner seeking an adrenaline rush.

Someone didn't know how close they came to this being their last day on earth.

41

"Clodagh—"

"Mrs McClintock you ignorant ba—" The woman rose from her seat.

Shona rose at the same speed, glared at the woman, and shouted. "Sit down. And stop with the swearing."

The woman thudded down, and the chair cracked. "This fu —" She took in Shona's face and said, "This crappy chair's going tae collapse on me." As if instructed the chair gave up its unequal struggle and threw its occupant to the ground. She landed square on her well-padded backside which barely left the seat of the chair. Cue more yelling. "I'll sue you lot." She turned to her lawyer, her face purple "Sue them."

Even Runcie had had enough. He frowned. "There's nothing wrong with you and it was your fault anyway. Let's just get this sorted and get out of here." He turned to Peter; "Can my client have another chair?"

"You're lucky we're not charging her for a new one the way she mistreated the one she got," said Shona

The lawyers look said give it in or I *will* find a way to sue you. Shona gave in gracefully, sighing deeply. *What a flaming case and what a flaming day. I need a new job.*

"Peter, get our prisoner a new chair."

"No' at my age. I'll get somebody else to dae it."

"Whatever."

"A doctor. I want a doctor. This is police brutality."

Her lawyer whispered in her ear with the result that her mouth snapped shut. She folded her heavily tattooed arms, in full view due to the cut off Death Metal t-shirt, and glowered.

Shona, who'd gotten used to glowering looks and was now immune to them, just thanked her lucky stars that at least the woman was quiet. She thought longingly of coffee, cakes, and paracetamol. The perfect combination.

A rookie entered with a brand-new chair that looked as if it could withstand a severe battering and the interview restarted.

"Clo…" Shona caught herself before the woman mountain kicked off. "Mrs. McLintock, you have been arrested for assault to actual injury on a police officer and a member of the public."

The woman opened her mouth; Shona continued before she could utter one word. "But that's not why we wanted to speak to you in the first instance. I believe you're Seamus McLaren's cousin. Is that correct?"

"Aye, the weaselly we git's dead. How do you want to speak to me aboot it?"

Shona, understanding some of the words worked out the gist of the sentence. "I believe you have taken over his business interests?"

Runcie put his hand on Clodagh's arm, leaned forward and said, "My client doesn't need to answer that?"

"Whyever not? It's a perfectly valid, might I say innocent, question. Unless she has something to hide of course."

More glaring and glowering ensued.

"My client has nothing to hide."

"In that case, she may want to answer my question." Shona

leaned back in her chair then whipped forward again. The pair on the other side of the table shuffled back a panic stricken look on their faces. Shona added, "And make it quick. We'd all like to be out of here before tomorrow's breakfast arrives."

Clodagh said, her voice slightly hesitant, "Aye. Aye, he wis. Wit does it matter?"

There was a knock at the door and a uniform handed in a note. Shona read it, folded it slowly, placed it on the desk in front of her, looked at her prisoner, and said, "Because Seamus was dealing in some pretty deadly gear and he and five others are dead. You're the only common factor."

Clodagh turned to her solicitor, who was turning purple. "Wit's she on aboot."

Runcie opened his mouth, but Shona saved him the trouble.

"I'm saying we're keeping you in the cells while we investigate you for the murder of…" She reeled off the six names.

The woman leapt to her feet and headed in Shona's direction. "I never murdered naebody but I'm going to kill you for framing me for murder."

Even Runcie joined in to restrain her. Once they slammed her down into her chair, which thankfully held, she visibly deflated; anger was replaced by sobs.

"I've got weans. Who's gonna mind them after school?'

"Have you any relatives who can pick them up from school?"

"No." She snivelled her nose running as fast as the tears that poured down her face." I never did wit you're saying. I wouldnae kill anybody."

"If that's the case our investigations will exonerate you."

"Wit are you on aboot?"

Runcie stepped in this time. "She's saying you'll be found not guilty." The solicitor' shoulder's slumped and he hung his head.

Shona had a feeling he was regretting this one.

He rallied and sat up straighter, his back ramrod straight. "I need to speak to my client given the latest turn of events."

"Of course." She turned to Clodagh, "We have a search warrant for your flat. Would you like to give us the keys? That will save us battering the door down."

Clodagh handed them over without a word and Shona said softly, "I'll make sure your children are cared for."

"Thanks." Her face relaxed and a small smile turned up one corner of her mouth.

No one was all bad, thought Shona. *Even pushers had a soft side and loved their children. Or murderers if it came to that.* She idly wondered what she would do if she was desperate to feed her kids. Those presently non-existent kids, thank God. She had enough on her hands with saving Christmas.

42

When they returned to the office, Nina and Abigail were heading out to search Clodagh's flat. "The warrant's just come in," said Nina.

"Hang on, I'll join you. Peter, can you get social services involved to look after Clodagh's kids?'

Nina drove as Abigail still didn't have a car and neither of them trusted Shona's driving.

"My mum wants me round hers for Christmas dinner," said Nina.

"I thought you were Hindu; do you celebrate Christmas?"

"We celebrate everything in our house. Any excuse for gathering her large and loving family to her bosom."

"Your mother's bosom aside, I'm not sure any of us will be scoffing Christmas dinner. We'll still be chasing a killer."

"I thought you had her in a cell," said Abigail.

"Keeping her out of the way while we search. We need evidence or Runcie will have her out of chokey quicker than we threw her in."

She pulled out her phone and dialled. Mary, I know this is unorthodox, but I need you to join us at…" She rattled off the address. "Your expertise is needed and, for once, I don't think it involves a dead body."

Clodagh's gaff was situated at the top of the Perth Road, a flat that took over one storey of a ginormous Victorian house, bult by the mill owners to house their ever-expanding families.

"I'm giving up policing and going into pushing," said Nina. "It obviously pays better than the way I'm earning a crust."

"Every career pays better than our monthly wage packet when you consider the hours we work," said Shona. "You're right though. How could she afford this pile of bricks and mortar?"

I wonder if she inherited this as well as her cousin's business?" Abigail pulled her phone out. "Shall I put Roy onto a background search."

Shona nodded. "Yep."

They rang the doorbell and waited. Nothing. She wouldn't put it past Clodagh to have left someone lying in wait for them. Nina unlocked the door and pushed it open. The flat may have been expensive but the inside looked like a hoarder's paradise and the smell hit them like a Harry Lawson truck.

"Wait for uniform to turn up. I've asked for help."

A few minutes later a squad car appeared, followed closely by Mary's Toyota Prius, the pathologist's attempt at being more environmentally friendly.

One of the police officers handed them all scene of crime overalls. Whilst this wasn't a scene of crime it wouldn't do to contaminate any potential evidence. Plus, who knew what they'd come up against in here.

They stepped inside and Shona told them to wait while she did a quick reccy. Returning, she briefed them, allocated them rooms and asked Mary to join her in the search. "You are literally the only person here who knows what this drug looks like."

Her gaze swept the others. "Be careful and don't touch anything that looks like drugs. Call for myself and Mary. I don't want to add police officers to the death toll.

"We didn't know you cared," said Abigail, grinning.

"Too much paperwork."

Nina took a deep breath and said, "This is going to be a hard slog. Are there any haystacks with needles in them available?"

"Less whinging and more searching if you don't mind."

They split up and so began the laborious process of searching what looked like the local midden.

43

Two hours, five bottles of water, and one fed up detective inspector later, they stopped to discuss progress. So far, nothing to indicate a drug dealer was in residence never mind a killer. Nor someone with a Christmas Vendetta, in fact, the cheeriest thing in the flat was the Christmas tree which towered up to the high ceiling.

"I'm still convinced she's got something to do with this," said Shona. "But how can we prove it."

Mary, a hesitant tone in her voice, said, "A friend of mine lived in one of these flats; let me try something." She scuttled through to the large sitting room, the others in hot pursuit, and hurried to the large, ornately engraved fireplace. She poked, prodded, shoved and twisted various parts of the engravings. "Maybe I've got it wrong," she muttered, and carried on with the task.

Five excruciating minutes later and a small section of the wall moved.

"Well, I'll be…" Shona's eyes and mouth were wide Os of astonishment. The others mirrored her expression.

"My friend kept wine in hers."

"I don't get the impression our Mrs McClintock is a wine connoisseur. I'll bet you all a round of drinks this space is stuffed to the gunnels with drugs."

No one took her up on the offer.

"Mary, you and I can go in first. You guys wait out here."

"How come you get to have all the fun," said Nina.

"Perks of the job." She hunkered down and slithered through the opening. The tiny Mary barely had to bend.

44

Hurrying inside the house the figure pulled out the package and locked it firmly in a drawer. Next, they sent a text:

Gear staying here. Get more locally.

Innocuous enough that no one would pick up on the deadly nature of the gear in question. Then, they opened a laptop followed by a browser and typed in flights to the U.S.A.

The phone pinged. A text:

Difficult to source here. Bring.

Anger in every tap, they sent a reply.

Source it.

Switching off the phone completely, they carried on with the task in hand. There was no time to waste. Phase three having now been brought forward there were plans to make.

45

Shona and Mary stood stock still which was pretty much the only way they could stand in a room so miniscule it was hardly worth the effort.

"Damn, I wasn't expecting this." Shona waved her hand emphasising the space.

"You didn't need me then?" Mary was decidedly chipper for someone who'd been dragged out unnecessarily.

"Looks like it."

"It's been quite exciting though, and I'm quiet at the moment. You've not sent me too many bodies." She grinned and added, "Yet."

"Ha, flaming ha."

Rather than being rammed floor to ceiling with drugs the room contained nothing but a small desk, a chair, and a laptop.

"No wonder our Clodagh was so quick to hand over her keys. There's nothing here." She stepped outside and hollered to Abigail who'd wandered off with Nina. "If you fancy doing a bit of work, grab a large evidence bag from the car. She turned back then halted. "Also, get the drug guys and forensics down here. I want this place tested head to toe for illegal substances and blood."

With the laptop safely deposited in the evidence bag, Shona said her farewells to Mary. "I've a sneaking suspicion we'll need you again, so don't stray far."

"I'm at your beck and call as always, Shona."

"Abigail, you stay and oversee what's being done. Nina, the car beckons."

Having quickly logged the laptop in as evidence Shona ordered Roy to put some gloves on and shoved it into his hands. "They'll be along to dust it for prints and check for drugs residue."

"Okay. I've enough to be getting on with anyway."

"You're not getting off that lightly. I want a forensic analysis of the inside of that computer. Stat."

"But—"

"Stat." She turned to Nina. "Find out where Roy is on his trawl for all things Clodagh McClintock and take over."

Moving to her office she pulled up all the files and images from the case so far. Here head spinning she thought of all the loose threads. Why Christmas? Why Christians? Why those victims? Where did VFE come in? Actually, where *did* VFE come in? She hadn't heard a dicky bird from Valerie Dickenson. She opened a drawer, fished around, pulled out the woman's business card, and dialled the number.

"Shona, I was going to call you later. I've three lecturers down with the flu and I'm doing four people's work."

"Have you got a few minutes now?"

"Sure, I've just stopped for a sandwich. I've made some enquiries and VFE Dundee Branch died about two years ago."

Shona's gob was well and truly smacked. "Died? Well now

it's resurrected. Why does that not surprise me? Christmas, santas, wise men, voodoo and now a spot of Easter in the form of a resurrection."

"It's a puzzle all right."

"You're telling me. Any chance you could scare up a name for me. Any blast from the past feelings?"

"I've barely a second to remember my own name but I'm always up for helping Scotland's finest. Let's see what I can do for you."

"You are a doll, Valerie. All help gratefully received, and I owe you a drink when this is all over."

"Make it a Bushmills and I'll double my efforts. My feelers are out as we speak."

"Shona had a feeling they were going to become good friends.

Her stomach reminded her that breakfast was long gone, and dinner was galloping towards her, so she headed for the canteen to see if there was something stodgy that would keep body and soul together. Her collapsing from low blood sugar wasn't going to move the case forward in any way and she could think just as well in the canteen over a plate of chips as she could in her office.

Unfortunately, whilst the stodge fortified her it failed to work its magic in any other way; her brain still ached, and she was still stumped. The deafening silence from the main office told her there was nothing to be gleaned from their activities either. The case defied all logic. Clues were conspicuous by their absence and the only witness was a small child with a vivid imagination. Whilst his English teacher probably loved him, he wasn't much help to her.

. . .

Hammering on her door and a figure bouncing through the opening startled her from her reverie. "Roy, this is a police station not the local playpark. When will you grow up?" She put her hand over her heart. *I'm getting too old for this.*

Roy, grinning, brought a glimmer of news. Whether it was good or not remained to be seen. "I've cracked it."

"I hope you're talking about the case." A hopeful smile twitched at the corner of her lips.

"Nope. The code to getting into Clodagh's laptop."

Before Shona could respond, Nina's designer clad figure appeared in the office, her Jimmy Choo heels tapping a staccato rhythm on the laminate flooring. "You'll never believe it. I—"

"Would the pair of you sit down." Shona put her computer to sleep and turned to the pair. "Roy, go for it."

"I'm into the deepest darkest depths of Clodagh's computer. She, or someone she knows is a computer wunderkind as it's locked down tighter than a Scotsman's sporran." He stopped and looked at Shona.

"Are you looking for praise and adoration. Consider it given."

He continued. "This was buried under numerous names and subsidiaries, but it looks like she owns one of the units in Dryburgh Industrial Estate. An extremely large one."

"Now you get the adoration." She turned to Nina. "Over to you before we go off on a raid."

"Turns out our Clodagh isn't as rough and ready as she sounds. The woman has a PhD in Chemistry."

"A real one or bought off the internet."

"Real as they come. I checked with her uni."

"Drug dealing obviously pays better than the chemistry gig." Shona clapped her hands. "Or it's needed to develop designer drugs. Let's set ourselves up a raid."

. . .

The mechanics of said raid took longer than first thought. Especially when it also involved the formerly known Scottish Drug Enforcement Agency which was now incorporated under the banner of Police Scotland. Even one big happy family had its rules and regulations. The raid was planned for the next night when most things would be shut up tight. With Clodagh tucked up in a cell and all those involved sworn to secrecy it would keep for twenty-four hours. Shona just had to cool her heels.

She grabbed her coat, dashed into the office, and was about to release them from the salt mines when she saw several children. All wearing grey school uniforms, the girls with tartan skirts." The trademark uniform of a private school.

"What the..." She took in Peter's sheepish face. "Care to enlighten me."

"These are Clodagh's bairns. We're trying to locate a relative."

Shona took a deep breath, decided not to explode, and chewed her lip. "What about Seamus's sister? She seemed fairly normal."

The oldest girl, who looked about fourteen and had a small child on her lap, said, "That's Auntie Morag. She'll take us." The little one sucked her thumb and cuddled into her sister. Four others sat on chairs next to them. Each sported a look of resignation. Obviously, a regular occurrence. Despite this they were all immaculately turned out and spotlessly clean. It looked like Clodagh, despite her life choices, cared for her children and wanted something good for them.

"I'm trying to get hold of her but apparently she's at work. I've sent Abigail to Ninewells to fetch her. "She's a nurse."

"I'll stay here with them, the rest of you are released from your shackles and can return to the warm bosoms of your families. Be back here bright and breezy at cock crow."

She turned to the children. "Come with me, we'll find some-where comfy to sit and I'm sure there are some doughnuts the gannets have left."

The kids perked up at this and the eldest rounded them up. Shona led them, like a mother duckling with her brood, in the direction of sustenance.

About an hour later she was child free and heading for her own sustenance in the form of the promised meal with her mother. She lacked the energy for it, but she needed to eat and someone else providing and paying for said food was a bonus.

46

The next day brought no new bodies, no new clues and much more hurry up and wait than Shona would have liked. Interviews with friends and families of the victims threw up nothing. More desperate chats with the evangelical churches shed no new light on the proceedings. Not did investigation of said churches. Everything was on the up and up and the victims were all upstanding citizens apart from the slimy David Brennan and Seamus, the drug dealer. It seemed like whoever killed those two would be given the freedom of the city and a parade. Even David Brennan's mother thought the world was better off without him. Peter et al spent the day trying to link Clodagh to any of the victims other than Seamus but drew a blank. According to family, friends, and colleagues, none of them did drugs. This case was beyond frustrating.

The boss called her into his office.

"I'm sorry, I didn't mean to wind him up, but the very look of him riles me."

"What are you on about, McKenzie?"

She stared right at him as her mind whirled. "You haven't had a complaint about me?"

His eyes narrowed. "No. Why, should I have done?"

"Not at all, Sir. How can I help you?"

"I want a briefing on tonight's outing with the drug boys."

She let out a breath. "Of course." She gave him chapter and verse of the operation. "So, I'm hoping we find evidence of the murders as well as drugs."

"Very well. That will be all."

As she walked out the door he called after her. "Keep that blasted DC of yours away from any accidents."

She wondered if he could have an accident. Preferably one that left him dead. Maybe Clodagh would oblige.

As the time for the raid approached, they all grabbed stab vests and made sure they were donned and tightly fastened. Everyone was issued with guns, despite them not being issued as standard in Police Scotland. Shona's team all had specialist firearms training as did the drug team. They piled into several police vans which were pointed in the direction of the industrial estate. Strictly speaking, Shona and her team weren't needed but she had an ulterior motive.

As she wasn't the lead on this, she spent the transport time briefing her team. "I want every single tiny room searched for any evidence of blood or a place where bodies could be stored and butchered. If Clodagh's a cold-blooded killer, I want to know about it."

"Shall we split into pairs? asked Peter.

"Good plan." She reeled off pairings, finishing by saying, "Jason, you're with me. I'll try and keep you in one piece.

. . .

The raid was both textbook and fruitful. In a drugs sense. Outside, a pristine blue sign sported the name River Tay Pharmaceutical Supplies. They battered down the doors and entered at speed. The drugs boys fanning out in a perfect formation. Inside the place had one large room of genuine supplies and the remainder of the, equally large, rooms were stacked floor to vaulted ceiling with designer drugs of every ilk including, according to Mary who had met them there, a large supply of Gu. The illicit drugs were efficiently catalogued and packed into the waiting vans and were soon heading for lockup in Bell Street.

Adanna Okifor appeared like a rabbit from a hat and asked for a statement. Shona, said, "Do you ever sleep?" before handing her over to her contemporary in uniform. He could deal with the reporter. "He'll tell you all you need to know."

He glared at her but chatted politely to the reporter. Shona was glad the raid would be all over the newspaper tomorrow and her investigation left out of it.

What they didn't find anywhere within the building was a body dump or a place that could be used to separate bodies and heads. Shona was fast coming to the conclusion that Clodagh might be a drugs king pin, but she wasn't their murderer. Not unless they found evidence somewhere.

Disappointed, she wound her weary way home. While she drove, she rang Douglas on hands free. She needed to hear his voice, which worked its soothing magic. Her bones weary, she idly wondered if she would be able to do this job for much longer.

Shakespeare, a cat of many moods, was in a particularly affection mood when she returned home, rubbing against her leg and meowing fit to burst. Her mother was still in residence, as was Fagan. They all appeared delighted to see her.

"There's a cheese platter awaiting your attention in the sitting room."

"You're a saint."

"I would have to be given I raised you and your siblings."

Shona cut off a chunk of creamy brie, served just at the right temperature, and slathered it on what looked like a Fortnum and Masons cracker. She bit into it and allowed the tastes to dance a tango on her tongue. She moaned, chewed, and picked up another cracker, this time choosing a blue cheese. "You'd definitely have to be a saint to raise Blair."

Her mother's laugh rolled around the flat. Fagan leapt up and ran over to her mother who fondled his ears. It was his turn to moan. Shakespeare merely twitched one of her ears, opened one eye, then returned to the serious business of sleeping.

This slice of normality soothed all her troubles away and all thoughts of dead bodies and Christmas being ruined sailed away on a cloud of comfort as did the feelings she needed a new job. It wasn't a career change she needed, it was her mother to move in and look after her for the rest of time. No matter how old you are, mum always makes things better.

47

F eelings of Comfort and Joy disappeared faster than snow in hell when she saw the next morning's newspaper. "I'm going to kill her." There wasn't a mention of the drugs raid on the front page. Another lurid headline took up prime space.

"Which unfortunate soul has got up your humph today, Ma'am?"

"Would you flaming well speak English." She lobbed the paper at him. "Odanna Okifor of course."

Peter peered at the front page of *The Courier*, the headline of which read Killing Christmas. The remainder of the article pretty much outlined the fact the police were a useless bunch of tossers who couldn't catch a cold in a blizzard.

Ignoring the headline and zeroing in on another important fact, Peter said, "You might be a wee bit hasty, Ma'am. You'd be killing the wrong person."

"Why?" She snatched the paper back and glared at it.

"Yon article was written by Gillian Cousins."

She handed the paper back and stomped off to ring Adanna. She was going to get to the bottom of this crass act of so-called journalism if it was the last thing she did.

. . .

"I'm as surprised and annoyed as you, Shona. In fact, I'm furious."

"Where did it come from? We agreed to keep this out of the press."

"Unfortunately, the grieving relatives didn't. They think you lot are dragging your heels, so they picked up a phone and dialled us. Gillian picked it up and ran with it. She'd murder her granny if she thought it would lead to a story, jumped up ignorant little git that she is. She'll literally run with anything."

"I'll be running her right out of town. This is all I need."

"I'm right there with you. I'm going to pitch a counter story to my boss giving your side of the story."

"What—?"

"Only if you're up for it of course."

"I'll speak to my boss." She stabbed at the red button on her phone and threw it on the desk. She wondered if she could get meditation classes on the firm's dime. All this stress must be playing havoc with her blood pressure.

The chief, as Shona had suspected, was singularly unimpressed with this turn of events. He read the article through. Thoroughly. And slowly. Shona shuffled but kept quiet. For once in her life, she wasn't sure what she should say.

He looked up and said, "You'd better call a press conference." He looked her up and down and said, "I'll front it. You come with me."

Shona suspected she'd been told off in an understated sort of way. She mentally shrugged her shoulders and thanked her lucky stars she didn't have to front the world's press. What an absolute load of old Horlicks this was turning out to be. She was looking forward to seeing the spin the Chief would put on this one.

The chief, suited and booted in his finest dress uniform, put on a show worthy of an Oscar. Shona, dressed in the smartest civvies she could muster at short notice, displayed an equally impressive image as she stood at his side. Scotland's finest in all their professional glory. Shona was in awe as she listened to the boss speak.

"I, on behalf of Police Scotland, would like to acknowledge the pain that the relatives of the recent victims must be going through right now. While such pain is regrettable at any time of the year, the fact it is Christmas must make this doubly agonizing. We currently have a killer in our midst who is striking at the very heart of Christmas. It is for this reason we have chosen to undertake our investigations quietly, and without alerting the public, as we did not want to cause unnecessary distress to the people of Dundee and Angus. This does not mean we are not taking this case seriously. I would like to reassure the families involved that we are doing everything in our power to bring the killer to justice and are currently pursuing several lines of enquiry. If anyone has any information which could help us in the case, please ring Detective Inspector Shona McKenzie on..." He rattled out the number and said, "That will be all for now." He turned and walked back into the station.

Shona was, once more, reminded why he was a Chief Inspector. Perhaps he wasn't quite so bad after all.

On returning to her office, Shona caught up with the findings from the previous night's raid. As she suspected, forensics showed there wasn't a drop of blood in the place. If Clodagh was the Christmas Killer, then she wasn't lopping off their heads in the same place she was designing drugs. Her finger-prints were all over the unit like measles. There was no way she was weaselling out of this one. Unless she had anything to do with Alexeyev one and three (two being in prison) in which case she'd be out of jail by teatime. The Russians were Teflon as nothing seemed to stick to them or their 'staff'. Talking of the Kalashnikov brothers, they seemed to have gone awfully quite recently. This worried her more than their usual interference. What were they up to that kept them away from the station?

Roy was earning a crust by searching for any link between Clodagh and the victims. He'd pretty much drawn blank. According to the socials, she was friends with a couple of them but not in a way that meant they met up, only through social media. This was unsurprising in Dundee – the biggest village in the world – where everyone knew everyone or at least had heard of them but no one knew anything that would help the police.

"I'm beginning to think Clodagh has nothing to do with our murders. She's supplying the Gu though."

"Seems that way. Might be worth interviewing her about her clients."

"Is there nothing in her laptop about that?"

"Detailed spreadsheets on every drug she manufactures and supplies."

"Fantastic. Haul in all the relevant people."

"I'm sure the drugs cops will be all over it like a rash. It doesn't help us though. Not one record mentions Gu." He took in her deflated posture. "Nor Jincan, which is its other name."

Shona sighed, squared her shoulders and said, "Get her into an interview room."

48

The change of plan brought all the kills into sharp focus. The flight was both quiet and uneventful giving them thinking time to plan their next move. Although the sudden change in plan was unexpected, it opened up whole new avenues. A frisson of excitement tingled down their spine. Taking a sip of a crisp rosé that had been served with lunch they jotted down notes in their trademark hardback black notebook. A fresh one with nothing in it to incriminate. The second glass of rosé found them drawing a detailed map using a mixture of memory and a guidebook. Still nothing to incriminate.

There were no nosy neighbours to sneaky beak what they were doing and no inane chatter. Business class made sure of that. The sketch was detailed, outlining everywhere they would need to go. Symbols were drawn, marking places the importance of which would be known to only a select few. These details were important from the past, but few would now know these details. Only the elect, those in power, those with power still remembered the old ways. The voodoo gods still spoke to them from beyond the grave. Every step they took was willed by the gods and they obeyed.

Finishing the map, they softly closed the notebook and placed the elastic snuggly around it. They placed it safely in the briefcase under the chair. Then, they reclined the chair and closed their eyes. They needed to be fresh on their arrival in the big easy.

Their eyes opened again within a few moments. Their heart raced as they thought about the Jincan they would collect in New Orleans. This rare poison could not be brought through customs. It had to be sourced locally. Anger burned in their heart as they thought of the person waiting for them in the bayou. This laziness, this disregard for the proper way that these things should be done, would not be tolerated. Taking slow deep breaths, they lay back once more and succumbed to slumber.

49

S hona once more found herself in an interview room facing Clodagh. This time the woman was much more subdued.

"Are my weans, okay?"

"They're fine. Seamus's sister has taken them under her wing."

"Aye. She'll be good to them until I get oot."

Shona slapped a file down on the table. "Stop with the poor wee Scottish lassie act. We know you've got degrees up the ying yang."

Little Miss Belligerent returned as quickly as the false accent left. "So, what. The last time I looked it's not a crime to be well educated."

"No. But the last time I looked it was a crime to be running a drugs empire."

"You're rather fanciful." The woman lounged back and studied her nails. She looked up and said, "When am I getting out of here? I've children to collect."

"In about twenty years. I think that's the going rate for manufacturing designer drugs, drug smuggling, and possession with intent to sell."

"You should write novels." The woman's laughter bounced off the walls.

"Is that right? Then my book would start with we found your laptop, have scoured it forensically, and found the address of your manufacturing plant." She watched as Clodagh's face cycled through every shade of pale. "Oh, did I say we raided it last night and we've enough evidence to put you away for a long, long, long time."

This time Clodagh's face cycled through the green palette as the knowledge of her future sank in.

"Unless of course you help us with our enquiries."

Clodagh sat up straighter. "I'll do anything. I've got to get out for my kids."

"I'm in the middle of a murder enquiry. I'd rather like your help for that."

Despair washed over her face. "I keep telling you, I've not murdered anyone."

"That's a matter for debate given the number of addicts that have died using your drugs."

"I don't know anything about your murders."

"We need to know who you've sold Gu to?"

"Isn't that chocolate mousse? How can that kill anyone? Seriously, you lot are barking."

"It's also a rare Chinese poison. You might know it as Jincan."

"You might as well be speaking Chinese." She leaned forward. "Honestly, I've no clue what you're on about."

Shona took a gamble. "Your cousin was killed by the poison. And it appears he was dealing it. We found some in your factory."

"I swear on my kids' lives I have no clue what you're talking about. Seamus was in and out that factory all the time. He must have left it there."

Shona looked at Roy. His look said I think she's telling the truth. Her look agreed.

"Have you got access to Seamus's records?"

"If the miserable snotbag kept any they'll be at his mother's flat."

"Address?"

The woman rattled it off and then added, "Can I see my lawyer?"

"Of course. I'll tell him you've been helpful."

She'd no sooner grabbed a coffee, her first of the morning, when she was told the Alexeyevs were waiting to see her. "Why am I not surprised. Tell them I'm busy and I'll be about twenty minutes."

She took her coffee to the main office and updated them on the latest developments. "Nina and Roy, go to the mother's house and do a search. Ring and get a warrant."

"If he lived with his mother, how come his sister reported him missing?"

"Who the heck knows. Haven't you noticed there's not one thing in this case makes any sense whatsoever. It makes our earlier cases look like we did nothing but join the dots."

"You're a laugh a minute, Shona," said Nina grabbing her coat.

"It's, Ma'am, to you," Shona shouted at her sergeant's retreating back. As usual no one paid a blind bit of attention leaving her with the feeling she'd lost all control. "They need sorting out," she muttered. Her tone held little conviction.

Whilst Roy and Nina headed off on a search, she headed off to chat to the Chuckle Brothers.

"What do you pair want now?"

Why are you persecuting us?" She thought it was Stefan as there was less glowering, but she couldn't be sure.

"Same old, same old. Come on Bill and Ben. We'll find a room for yet another wee chat."

"Who is this Bill and Ben of which you speak?"

"Never mind." She pushed open the door to an interview room and ushered them in. "Would you like a tea or a coffee." This was more to do with her caffeine levels than being nice to the terror brothers.

"Russian tea."

"We've got Tetley's. Do you want milk in it or not?"

"No. Lemon." More glowering ensured, she assumed at her failings in the beverage department.

"Two black teas, coming up."

She poked her head out and asked a passing copper to grab one of her team and ask them to bring the beverages and themselves to the interview room. Five minutes of threatening looks and crossed arms later, Iain appeared with the order.

"There is no lemon. We asked for lemon."

"Hard luck, sunshine, this is a police station; we're more greasy spoon than The Ritz. Now, what do you want?"

The Russian took an infuriatingly long sip of his drink and did a spot more glaring.

Shona sat up higher and did some glaring of her own. "That's enough. Either spit it out or ship out."

"I not understand what you are say." Shona figured out this was Igor as his English wasn't quite up to snuff.

"I'm saying tell me why you wanted to talk to me or leave." She leaned forward and slammed the desk with her hand. "I'm in the middle of a murder investigation here and don't have time for this."

Her posturing did nothing for the Russian brothers. The only sign of anger was a small twitch at the corner of Stefan's piercingly blue left eye. He obviously managed to restrain himself, given he was in a police station; he spoke without a hint of menace in his voice. "You have one of our employees in custody."

Shona's heart sank knowing just where this was going. "Who would that be?"

"Clodagh—"

"Before you say anything else you might want a lawyer present."

"Why do we need a lawyer? We have done nothing wrong."

"Given the nature of Clodagh's arrest."

"She is a cleaner. This is not against the law in our country. Is it here?"

"She's been arrested on drug charges."

"Of this we know nothing."

Damn weasels have wriggled out of things again. "We will not be releasing your employee any time soon. I suggest you find another cleaner. Dundee's awash with them. I could recommend a terrific one. Goodbye gentlemen."

The Russians stood, did a bit more glowering, and were escorted off the premises by Iain.

Shona gathered up the cups and headed in the direction of the kitchen and then the Chief. She practiced a bit of glowering in case she needed to employ it when speaking to the chief.

Despite the china teacup of Earl Grey and a couple of rich butter shortbread, the Chief's favourite biscuits, which she deposited on his desk, he refused to allow her to get a search warrant for the Alexeyev's home. "How many times do I have to tell you, they are respectable businessmen. Are you deaf?"

"They're employing McLintock, I'd say that means they are up to their unrespectable Slavic necks in dirty deeds."

"It is not illegal to employ a cleaner."

"She's a drugs kingpin and a pusher." Shona crossed her

arms and tapped her foot. "The only thing she's cleaning is other people's problems."

"Alleged kingpin and pusher." He looked at her his grey eyes a no-nonsense steel. "Less of the attitude and go and solve this bally case. Preferably without more victims.""

She was once more looking at the Chief's bald head and summarily dismissed.

She left wondering what it would feel like to stuff him full of hallucinogens and watch how it played out.

S hona arrived back in the office to the shrill sound of a ringing phone. She grabbed it hoping it was a break-through in the case, disappointment surged through her when she realised it was just her mother. She gave herself a mental kick – ordinarily she would be delighted to hear from her loving parent.

"I'm booked on the sleeper to London tonight. I'm meeting your father there for a few days seeing the sites."

"Lucky you. I can say my fond farewells tonight."

"That's why I'm ringing. We can have dinner out again."

She hung up wondering why her mother didn't want anything to do with her cooking. It wasn't that bad. She also wondered what she was going to do with the always lively Fagin. Her neighbour would be putting her flat up for sale if she was dumped with him for much longer. She idly wondered if anyone fostered dogs for a living and decided the minute she had five seconds without a dead body on her hands, to look it up.

. . .

Nina and Roy returned and presented themselves in her office with a file in their hands and a tale of horror on their lips.

"That poor woman is completely out of it. Alzheimers," said Roy.

"I'm not sure anyone's been looking after her since Seamus met his grisly end," added Nina. "The poor soul was in a right state."

"We had to break in."

"What?"

"Relax, Shona. Emergency. We saw her lying on the hallway floor."

"Where is she now?"

"Ninewells in the care of both paramedics and social services." Roy rubbed his hands over his eyes. "I hope to God my mother never ends up like that."

Shona felt sick that an elderly woman could be so neglected in this day and age. She squeezed her eyes shut, opened them, and said, "Good job for getting her sorted." She pulled the folder towards her. "I take it these are our Seamus's records."

"Seems like it." Nina tucked her hair behind her ears. "Although they're a right mess."

"Both of you sit down. We'll divvy them up and analyse every word."

Roy groaned. "Does it involve a computer?"

"No, it flaming well doesn't." Shona threw a pencil and paper at him. "Drag yourself back to the stone age and get working."

Roy groaned again.

Shona wasn't in the mood for histrionics. "Suck it up."

Bending their heads, they applied themselves to the task. Pages were turned, notes made, and the clock ticked. An hour later, Shona turned the last page on her not insignificant pile, stretched, and rubbed her back. The others sat back.

"Well," asked Shona. "Are we any further forward? Findings? You first Roy."

"If he was alive and kicking, he'd be a doing a long stretch for dealing, but not a word about Gu or Jincan."

She turned to Nina. "What about you?"

"Good news and bad. Which do you want?"

"Just spit it out. I'm growing old here."

"He was definitely dealing Jincan. To one client."

Shona made a victory sign. "Get in there. A breakthrough at last." Her grin could light up the Dundee Christmas Tree.

"Err. Not quite. We've no name. Just a number."

"What? From a Dundee dealer? I feel like I'm in the middle of a spy novel." Her mouth turned down as she sighed. "Another dead end." She chewed on her lip and then, straightening up, said, "He must have got the Jincan from someone. But who? Grab the others and interrogate every dealer and addict in the city. Somebody must know something."

"Look how well that worked out last time." Before Shona could react, he disappeared out of the door. Shona had to agree with him; forlorn and hope were the words that sprang to mind.

They'd no sooner left, and Shona turned her hand to working through a three-week pile of memos and reports, than a voice was heard.

"Have you got any cake, Shona."

Shona's head shot up, a smile splitting her face in two. She took in a blonde-haired, green-eyed imp in the form of a small child. This was her soon to be stepdaughter. "Alice! What brings you here?"

"Daddy's got a meeting with some 'portant person. He's the boss of the whole police in Scotland."

Blast, I didn't know the Chief Constable was in the building. Well. It sounds like he'd be in a meeting for the foreseeable, so plenty time for cake. She grabbed Alice by her perfectly cute hand and said, let's see what the gannets have left."

"Rory's the gannet in our house. He eats all the cake." Her tone held a hint of crossness of the type only small girls can conjure up.

"Rory's a teenage boy. They all eat a lot because they're growing bigger." At least Shona thought that was the case. Never having had much to do with teenage boys since she left school, she wasn't actually that sure. Still, it sounded reassuring enough.

"Why aren't you at school?"

"Teachers have to learn something. Sounds boring."

Shona thought that just about summed it up. All adult jobs were fairly boring. Most of them weren't awash with dead bodies.

Shona found one forlorn chocolate eclair in the fridge. She was willing to give it to the child but her future stepdaughter insisted they share it; this boded well for their future relationship. Shona had an emergence stash of colouring books and pencils in her drawer, mainly because her station seemed to be awash with children at the oddest times. Shona worked and Alice coloured in companionable silence until Douglas accompanied the Chief Constable into her office.

"I'll take Mini the Minx here off your hands now," said Douglas.

Alice giggled. I'm not a minx, I'm a good girl."

Her father ruffled her hair and helped her on with her coat. "That you are, I'm sure you're on Santa's good list. Come on. We're having fish and chips for tea if you manage to get through the day without trouble." He cocked an eyebrow at Shona. "Any chance you can join us?"

"Not a fraction of a chance. Sorry. Too much work and I've to wish a fond farewell to my mother."

"I need a word with your fiancé anyway." The Chief Constable and Douglas shook hands and father and daughter went on their merry way." The Chief Constable sat down. "Can you update me on your latest case?" He smiled showing dazzlingly white, perfectly straight teeth.

Shona, thinking the Chief Constable gig must pay well to afford that level of dentistry, obliged him with the update.

"Is there any chance this will be solved quickly?" he said when she drew to a halt.

"With all due respect, Sir, not a hope."

"I thought you would say that. Is there anything I can do to help you?"

"At the moment, no. We're stalled."

"I believe our American colleagues have been in touch?"

"Yes, Sir. They're following our case with interest."

"Have they divulged why?"

"They had similar murders and then they stopped. They think their killer moved here." She paused and then added, hesitancy in her tone. "Actually, there is something you can do, Sir."

"Anything."

"Can you use your rank to pin down the names of some of the ex-members of a group called Voodoo for All?"

"Shona, your cases never cease to amaze me." He stood up. "Let me see what I can do." He smiled and added, "In the meantime, see if you can keep the body count down."

"Of course, Sir." *What does he bally well think I can do about it? The killer's not exactly asking my advice on whether he should dump another dead body on my patch.*

Five hours of foot tapping, finger drumming tension (on Shona's part) later, the others appeared back in the office. They were foot sore, freezing and grumbling like a pride of grannies at a jumble sale. Thankfully everyone appeared to be in one piece.

"Soldier boy, glad you haven't managed to fall at the latest hurdle and are still hanging in there with us."

Jason grinned. "I've turned over a new leaf."

"I very much doubt it. Now, what have you got for us? Peter, summarise."

"Every last druggy or dealer we interviewed looked at us as if we were talking Chinese. Looks like he got it from outside."

"Your choice of language isn't very PC, Sergeant Johnston."

"Aye, tell that to the people in the street."

Moving on from Dundee vernacular, Shona asked Abigail. "What's your take on it? Any insight into it from a Chinese point of view?"

"Not a thing. I can ring a couple of contacts in China to see if they've picked anything up on the grapevine."

"Solid stuff, thanks."

"They're seven hours ahead, so I'll have to wait until the morning."

"Okay, you're all free to flee the gulags and return to the loving and warm embrace of your nearest and dearest. There's nothing more for tonight."

They grabbed coats and stampeded towards the door; Shona headed for her office to write an email to her contemporaries elsewhere. Someone had to know something about Jincan as she was now calling it as Gu led to too many comments about chocolate pudding. Before she started, she sent a text to her mother telling her she would soon be finished and asking where they were meeting for dinner. If nothing else, she'd be well fed.

51

Shona woke to grey skies and fog, with a headache that could kill the bear up at Camperdown Park. There had been a few too many Taliskers quaffed during the dinner with her mother. On both their parts. She decided to take Fagin for a run in the hope it would clear her head. A brisk four miles would make or break her. Grabbing a refillable water bottle, she called to the hound. He bounded through, tongue lolling and pranced around her feet like Widow Twankie in the pantomime at Whitehall Theatre. Seriously, where did he get his energy from? Shakespeare opened one eye, threw them a look that said are you pair mad, and went back to the serious business of sleeping. Shona thought she might come back as a cat in her next life.

She and the canine thief presented themselves in the station. She managed to palm the mutt off on an unsuspecting secretary who liked dogs. She also deposited a lead, a couple of packets of dog treats and a dog poop bag. Fagin settled down under the secretary's desk and started to snore. Shona felt like joining him.

She called Abigail into her office. "Any joy with your contacts?"

"Being Chinese they weren't keen to spill the beans, but it would appear some of the stuff has been circulating recently. They've been a bit caught on the hoof as it's ancient and no one has heard of it in years."

"Any idea who's exporting it here?"

"They don't even know if anyone *is* exporting it here."

"No further forward then, though I'd bet my granny on the fact it is coming from China."

"Yep. Confucius would probably say you were right."

"Did he have anything to do with Jincan?"

"Not that I'm aware of. Not unless his sayings are even more profound than we think."

"Blast and damn. Will we ever get a break?"

Abigail took the easy way out by ignoring the question and scurrying off to her duties. She did, however, return with a large mug of fully loaded coffee and plonked it on Shona's desk. She figured the boss needed it.

Shona fired up her computer which, it being a top of the range Mac on steroids, did not take long. Every police force in the UK was in work at sunrise if the number of emails in her inbox were anything to go by. It proved her theory that UK policing was run by copious amounts of caffeine and very little sleep. She waded through them, force by sleepless force, but nary a one knew anything about Chinese drugs never mind ones that had fallen of the face of the earth long before any of them were a twinkle in their parents' eyes. She hadn't expected anything else to be honest, but it was still frustrating.

. . .

A phone call to Matt Hernandez in the New Orleans Police Department did nothing for the case but his voice, as previously, made her feel all was right with the world. There had been no further murders and nothing in their archives that could shed light on the matter.

"I've run it past every state here in the USA but drawn a blank at every turn, Miss Shona."

"Similar situation here. I thought my previous cases were hard, but this defies all logic."

"I'd heard you catch the weird cases. I thought it was only NOLA that attracted those."

"Apparently not. At least you're warm in New Orleans. We're usually freezing our assets here in Scotland."

"Maybe you'll get to come here and work with us in our fine city."

"Fat chance. The boss would throw a hissy fit at the thought."

"I hear ya. You have a nice day now, Ma'am, and I'll be in touch if anything crosses my desk that could shed some of our wonderful NOLA light on things."

"Thanks. Matt. Appreciated."

Shona took a large slurp from her freshly refilled coffee mug and set to with research on Marie Laveau and Voodoo. Maybe she'd get a handle on her followers by finding out about the woman herself. She spent an interesting couple of hours steeped in Louisiana history. Fascinating stuff.

She learned Marie Laveau was a free woman of colour who bore numerous children to both her husband and, after his death, a man with whom she entered into a domestic partnership. Herbalist and practitioner of voodoo, she acted like she owned the streets of New Orleans and very quickly became the queen of voodoo. However, it would appear she was also a practicing Catholic. Most interestingly, for Shona's investigations, was that Marie was often asked to attend to men before they went to the gallows following a sentence of death. Rumours abounded that many of the men were poisoned or were given potent medicines, however, this was never confirmed. Her daughter vehemently declared her mother merely prayed with the men in the Catholic tradition.

In Shona's mind, the issue was not whether Marie Laveau used poison or not, but whether the nutjobs at Voodoo For All believed she did. She was willing to bet Fagin (who was now mysteriously curled up at her feet) that they had leapt on this part of the equation. How they transferred this to Christmas icons remained a mystery. Shona was only thankful that all of Dundee's Christmas characters had remined alive for a couple of days.

She picked up the phone and dialled Valerie Dickenson. "Do you know anything about VFA following the more esoteric parts of Marie Laveau's reputed acts."

"Such as?

"Poisoning people to assist their death."

"Not that I've heard of, but I'm fairly sure your boy is doing so. Or girl, I suppose. A lot of Marie's followers are females."

"Never, say never when it comes to a killer's gender. This particular woman would need some strength though."

"Sounds like you're looking for an Olympic weightlifter."

"Nothing would surprise me. This case is all colours of madness."

"Good luck with it. I'm still doing some research for you and will be in touch if I come up with anything."

She briefed the team on the latest glimmer of a development but was at a loss as to where to go from there. For once in her career, she was out of options on the next step. She asked Roy to keep researching the deepest, darkest depths of the interweb and set the rest to solving a couple of cold cases. Maybe they'd crack them and find something about this case in the process. Dumb luck would seem to be the only thing that could help them now.

52

Four days later they were no further forward. The cold cases turned out not to be quite so cold after all. The individuals they'd thought were missing had returned to the joyful bosoms of their families several months later without anyone informing Police Scotland. Shona thought their lives in the police would be a lot easier if it didn't involve the general public. They'd had a couple of days where they had finished on time much to Douglas and the children's delight. Alice had declared Shona missed out on fish and chips, so they needed them again. Apparently, Shona's life would be over if she didn't have them. Thus goes the histrionics of a child. Her father, laughing, had agreed it might be a jolly good idea but no more until after Christmas. Shona thought, nce again, how lucky she was to have them in her life.

She'd no sooner taken off her coat, put her handbag away, and grabbed a cup of coffee, when the boss called her into his office.

"You're going to New Orleans."

Shona's mouth formed a perfect O. After several long

seconds she managed to utter, "Sorry, Sir, I thought you said I had to go to New Orleans."

"Are you deaf? That's exactly what I said." He frowned. "Our cousins across the pond have requested your presence to help with a case. Apparently, the Virgin Mary has turned up dead in their neck of the woods."

Shona swallowed. "What? How? When do I have to go?" Her voice had taken on a squeak of its own.

"Today. Go home and fetch your passport."

"But, Sir, it's Christmas."

"You seem to have forgotten that you're in the police. Far be it for me to interfere with your Christmas festivities." His voice dripped with so much sarcasm you could butter bread with it. "Pack a bag, or don't pack a bag, it's all the same to me. You're on a flight at 4 pm from Edinburgh to Gatwick. You'll pick up your connecting flight there."

Shona, never usually averse to a trip at the boss's expense, was devastated. This would be her first Christmas as a family, with Douglas and the kids. Well almost family, when they set a date for the wedding. She took a deep breath and said, "Am I going alone?"

"If you think you're off for a holiday with your boyfriend, think again. Sgt Johnston will be accompanying you. Please let him know."

This would not go down well. To Peter, a devout Catholic, Christmas was sacrosanct.

"Yes, Sir. Of course."

She left wondering if she could leave his headless corpse loafing in a wood. Preferably one closer to New Orleans than Dundee. Although, to be honest, she was rather thrilled that she was getting a trip to America at the firm's expense. She'd never thought of going to New Orleans but the more she researched it, the more she longed to go. It sounded amazing. It was also hot. And she'd meet Mr Sexy Voice. A win all round. Also, she was sure the Kalashnikov brothers would be nowhere near the city – an added bonus. Give or take the poor woman who had been murdered and the deaths of santas and wise men to solve, it sounded like a jolly good jaunt. Who was she to look a gift horse etc.

"I cannae go traipsing halfway around the world. The wife'll kill me."

"Then, I shall attend your funeral. Man up, it's the boss's orders."

"It'll be as hot as hell in the deep south."

"Yep, pack summer clothes."

"They're in the loft."

"Peter, quite frankly, I don't care if you turn up in a three-piece twill and a fur coat, or where your wardrobe is situated. Go home, say a fond farewell to the long-suffering Mrs Johnston and pack a bag. Or buy everything there." She waved an A4 sheet in front of his face. "Here's your ticket. Get the wife to drop you at the airport by 13.00."

"I'll take his place," said Nina. "N'Orleans is meant to be fabulous."

Not a hope in hell's chance. You'd be chatting up the natives and spending all your time in shopping malls. We've a killer to catch. That involves work."

"Spoilsport."

"Yep." Shona shrugged her shoulders.

She left the team sulking and went to break the news to the Procurator Fiscal that his top detective was off to the good old U.S. of A. She could just picture his devastation at the thought of her departing this close to Christmas. His take on it was that the body count would go down considerably once she stepped on the plane. Also, could she bring some American chocolate back for the kids' stockings. Sometimes she wondered why she agreed to marry him. His insouciance at her imminent departure didn't smack of love and devotion.

His parting shot was, "I'll phone the local sheriff's department and warn them their death rate is about to rocket skywards."

Shona hit end on her phone. He'd be lucky if he got a Christmas present other than her engagement ring back. She shrugged on her coat and went to dig out her own summer clothes, hoping she'd have a chance to do a spot of sightseeing. Researching The Big Easy had her raring to go. Chock full of special cemeteries, she might even be able to visit a dead body or two that didn't involve her investigating them. She rather liked to visit cemeteries around the world; there was something anchoring about them – a connection to the past. A reminder that not everyone who died did so under nefarious circumstances.

5 3

The flight from Edinburgh to London was swift and accompanied by a sandwich and a large coffee. It was also accompanied by Peter's grumbling which Shona mainly tuned out. The grumbling stopped once he did damage to a chicken wrap and a glass of McEwans Lager. Far be it for Peter to drink anything other than Scotland's best.

On arrival at Gatwick, Shona thought all her Christmases had come at once when she discovered the firm forked out for a business class fare for her. She idly wondered if they'd sacked someone to pay for it, the force not being known for its generosity.

Due to the last-minute booking, Peter was in premier economy. Either that or Police Scotland thought a Sergeant didn't merit a higher class of fare, but he was happy with his lot. This left her with little company. A tall woman, positively jingling with precious jewels, sat in the seat next to her, next being a relative term in business class. The woman removed her fur coat, hat and scarf and settled herself in for the journey. Shona wondered whether the fur was real. Probably necessary given the first leg of the journey was New York. Louisiana might be putting on a heatwave worthy of the height of summer, but New York was blanketed in three feet of snow. She only hoped they'd be able to land.

The woman accepted the proffered glass of Champagne. Shona had one as well. The few hour layover in New York would give a perfect buffer to sobriety. The woman leaned back and closed her eyes. Shona pulled out her book, one of several she'd bought at the airport and settled back. She'd already prepared to the nth degree with regards to working with the NOLA police, thus intended to make the most of her unexpected eight hours of freedom.

Later in the flight they met again at the bar. Yes, business class could share the bar with first class. Shona thought she could get used to this level of service. She grabbed a cheeseboard whilst the woman ordered more Champagne. Her new companion introduced herself. "Lucy Sylvester." Her accent was so cut crystal it could be used to pour whiskey. Shona shook the perfectly manicured hand, wishing she'd had time for a manicure herself. The sudden urge to laugh was strong. She really had met Lucy in the Sky with Diamonds.

"What takes you to New York?" asked Lucy.

"Layover to the deep south. Much as I'd love to see New York in all its wintry splendour, work beckons."

"At Christmas?"

"Quite. That's what I said to my boss. He wasn't having any of it. So, here I am, a slave to the machine."

Lucy opened her voluminous handbag and pulled out what looked like a solid gold business card case. Slipping a card out she handed it to Shona. "If you're looking for a new job, give me a call."

Shona glanced at the card which informed her Lucy was in the line of consulting services. Pushing down an urge to interrogate her new BFF, she slipped the card in the pocket of her jacket.

Her voice said, "Thanks. I'll bear that in mind." Her mind said, *once I've checked you out first. You've no clue who I am or what I do so what would make you think I'm a good fit for your consultancy business? Still, whatever it is, it pays jolly well if you're anything to go by.*

Back in her seat she used the free onboard Wi-Fi to send a message to Roy to check out the mysterious Lucy Sylvester. Then, she switched her phone off, leaned back in her seat and picked up her book. Whilst she read, she sipped another glass of Champagne and nibbled on a platter of mixed fruit while she waited for the main meal to appear. She felt a momentary guilt pang for checking out a woman she'd just met, then shoved it deep down. Mysterious strangers offering high paid jobs to random people at 30,000 feet deserved investigation. But her book, and the complimentary beverages and nibbles, deserved equal attention. She lost herself in fictitious crime stories set in New Orleans. *Maybe I'll pick up a tip or two. Lord knows, I need them. I'll use the New York layover to study all the notes in depth again. Now is the time to relax.*

The landing in New York was smooth and they were soon taxiing up to the runway. Shona stood up and collected her coat and bag from the overhead locker. Lucy bid her farewell and encouraged her to keep in touch. Shona found her luggage on the carousel and waited for Peter to grab his. Soon they were striding towards customs clutching the bottles of Whisky and tins of shortbread, purchased in duty free – gifts for their NOPD hosts. Scottish hospitality at its best.

. . .

The layover in New York was uneventful. Pete managed to have yet another meal and Shona took the opportunity to drink copious amounts of extra strength coffee and take another look at her files. She also bought a couple more novels and some Hershey goodies in one of the numerous gift and bookshops. She thought about buying some clothes until she looked at the price and quickly decided to give that idea a swerve. In the arrivals hall a fully uniformed officer, complete with gun, bore a crisply typed sign with their names. After a quick, "Welcome to N'Orleans, Y'all," they were whisked through the door. Peter immediately started wiping his brow with a handkerchief. Shona, a hothouse plant, thought she'd come home and could have kissed the ground. An air-conditioned police car, or cruiser as she was to find out it was called around these parts, awaited them. Bags were stowed in the trunk, the siren was switched on, and they sped towards the station in Broad Street. It was only 8pm in NOLA but 2am for the Scots contingent. As Peter, in the front seat, yawned and chatted to the American police officer, Shona took in the dazzling sights around her, even if they were whizzing by at warp speed. If she could even think about keeping her eyes open, she would be impressed; she'd forgotten to add jet lag into her highly excitable equation. Her thoughts had been more of the sun and more sun variety, with a soupcon of murder solving thrown in.

They had no sooner stepped in the front door of the station than a voluminous whirlwind approached. "Lordy, Lordy, you must be our Scottish guests. You are so welcome to our beautiful city. Give me some sugar." Shona found herself enveloped in a hug the size of Scotland. Peter took a step back, but he was next for the hug treatment. "I'm Trina, and if you need anything, anything at all now, you come and see me at the front desk."

Shona managed to recover her breath enough to mutter, "Of course. How generous, Trina."

Peter just stood looking dazed. Shona supposed he wasn't used to anyone other than his wife or daughter hugging him. He also looked like he was about to drop on his feet. Shona, taking one look at him, thought it was time for bed for the both of them.

They were ushered into Captain Hernandez's office. Every inch of his six-foot frame lived up to his sexy voice and Shona almost swooned. If she wasn't already taken, or him given the ring on his finger, this could be a match made in heaven.

"Welcome to our fine city, Inspector. Thank. y'all for coming to collaborate on catching this heinous killer."

"It was our pleasure. I'm not sure how useful we'll be tonight though. It's 4am for us."

"Of course, Where are my Southern manners. My mama would be tearing me a new one right now." He moved to the door and hollered, "Miss Trina, find me a driver."

Trina herself appeared. "Matt Hernandez, I'll be telling your mama about all this yelling. My boy will be here in five minutes."

Trina's boy deposited them in a grand hotel. They confirmed NOPD were paying, handed them key cards, and a porter showed them and their luggage to their rooms. Shona took one look, decided it looked great and was in the land of nod within ten minutes.

54

Due to the time difference Shona eyelids pinged open by 6 a.m. Switching on the lights she looked around the room. Very grand, it even had a coffee machine with capsules. Once she'd set the machine to brew caffeinated nectar, she took a peek out of the window. It was still pitch black, although the lights did look pretty. She'd asked for a newspaper to be delivered each day and with the expected American efficiency a local broadsheet loafed outside her door. She climbed back into bed, settled back and drank a couple of mugs of coffee while she caught up on the local news. The murder of the Virgin Mary was splashed across the front page in all its horrifying detail, yet tastefully done, in deference to the poor woman's family thought Shona. What that poor family must be going through. She glanced at her watch, leapt out of bed, and dialled Peter's room number.

He was awake. "Is breakfast included?"

"It sure is. I'll meet you in the foyer in half an hour."

She threw herself into the shower and washed every inch of her, shampooing her hair twice. All that travel followed by heat that hugged the body like a long lost lover left a girl feeling grubby. She flung on a pair of light trousers and short sleeved blouse, then opened the curtains to welcome the light. The sight took her breath away. The Mississippi River lay before her in all it's magnificent, shimmering splendour. Nothing prepared her for this. To complete the picture a paddleboat sailed into view. Shona stood and took it all in – mesmerised – before shaking herself, slipping on some shoes and heading to breakfast. She navigated the dizzying number of lifts, all of which seemed to stop at different floors, and made it to the foyer and headed into breakfast. The breakfast buffet was larger than The Mississippi, which fact kept Peter quiet and occupied for the next thirty minutes. Shona took the opportunity to ring Matt who said someone would be there to pick them up within twenty minutes. She also gave Bell Street a quick call but, apart from continuing jealousy, there was no news. She declined to tell them about her view, feeling that might lead to them planning her demise, possibly by drowning in the Mississippi or feeding her to the alligators in the Louisiana Bayou. She then turned her attention to a mound of pancakes higher than the Law Hill and wondered how far she could run in this heat.

They didn't do things by halves in New Orleans. A patrol car picked them up and deposited them two blocks up the road. They could have walked it. Peter moaned about the heat and Shona warned him if one more word about the weather came out of his mouth, he'd be on foot patrol for the rest of his career. Starting now. He opened his mouth, thought better of it, and snapped it shut again. Shona relished the warmth and had a stern word with God for inventing air conditioning.

55

I nside the station they were welcomed, given coffee, and measured up for stab vests and holsters.

"We don't need guns," said Shona. "Scottish police don't use them."

"I know y'all are weapons trained. Y'all will have the same dinky guns you use back home. Here in N'Orleans you'll be carrying." Matt had a look of a man who would not be argued with.

Shona gave in gracefully and she and Peter filled in all the relevant forms and trotted off to the shooting range to demonstrate their skills. She was thankful neither of them disgraced the force. They were soon suited up, weapons at their side and ready to go. Ready to go where she wasn't sure, as they were then given more coffee, and sat down for a briefing. Despite the fact it was all carried out with brisk efficiency, Shona was antsy – anxious to see some action. Peter, a tea drinker, had the look of a man who was going to the gallows. She whispered in a cop's ear, and he disappeared off returning with a mug of tea. Given its strength, Shona didn't think it would improve things much, but it was tea.

. . .

Matt took control with seamless efficiency and authority. His team hung on to his every word. Shona wondered if she could get some lessons on how to recreate this in her own team.

He pointed at a map.

"For the benefit of our Scottish visitors, this is Audubon Park in our historic district." His laser dot moved to an area inside the park. "The body was found on the Wisner Loop of the Nature Center." He stopped and swallowed. "It was discovered by an eight-year-old boy who was walking the trail with his family."

The room fell silent.

Tears in his eyes, Matt spoke again, a tremor evident in his voice. "The victim was a seventeen-year-old girl, identified as Savannah More. She was reported missing three days ago." As Matt continued his voice grew stronger and more business-like. "Her head was separated from her torso and replaced. Around her head were three red candles, with VFA engraved on a nearby tree."

Shona asked, "Did your previous victims have all the trappings?"

"No, Ma'am. Just the beheadings and the Christmas dress – Father Christmas, an elf, and someone in a reindeer sleepsuit."

"Escalating then. What's the plan of action?" It was time to move on and move forward before anyone else died.

"All in good time, Miss Shona. First, you need to know the park is locked overnight when it looks like the body was dumped. This means there's a good chance that whoever did this worked in the park."

"Could a previous employee have copied the key?"

"Anyone copying these keys would be reported to us."

Peter chipped in. "Aye, maybe that's right but I bet there's someone who'd do it off the books."

"Good point. Or someone could have stolen a relative's key."

"Y'all are making good suggestions and my officers are on all of those scenarios." He shut down his laser pointer and popped it in his pocket. "Let's hit the crime scene and then I'm taking you to a voodoo museum."

"Did he say a voodoo museum," said Peter sotto voice. "Have we got time to be playin' tourists?"

"He must have his reasons." Inside even she wondered what was going on but decided to trust her American colleague.

She stood up, adjusted her holster and gun so it felt marginally more comfortable and stepped out into sunshine so bright it burnt your retinas. She pulled out her sunglasses and popped them on, thanking the fates that she was somewhere hot. Then she felt guilty because of the reason she was here and turned her mind to murder.

56

They were deposited at the gates to the park and had to walk the remainder of the way. The temperature flirted with 28 degrees or 82 degrees in American terms. In, Dundee, a city where 18 was considered a heatwave, temperatures like this drove the population mad. In New Orleans, the day was considered a little chilly. Shona and Peter had sweat rolling down their faces. Matt Hernandez looked calm, cool and collected as he strode through the park's 350 acres. Shona, struggling to keep up, thought she'd worked off every calorie laden bite of her breakfast. Even she was grateful to be inside a tent that covered the crime scene. The body was long gone but the police investigation continued. Someone thrust coveralls in their direction and Peter groaned as he donned them. All credit to him he didn't complain.

Once suited up, Matt led them on a walk around the scene. "Thoughts so far?" he asked.

"When was the last rainfall?"

"About four months ago?"

"So, everything's bone dry. Any indication they'd dragged the body? Any blood? Any footprints? Tyre Marks?"

"Yes, to the dryness of the terrain. No, to everything else. Except the footprints, "Y'all know how many footprints there are in a public park now, Miss Shona."

"Yep. It's like looking for a needle in a thousand haystacks. Anything you could use for DNA?"

"No, although there was a very small piece of cloth hanging on a fallen tree branch. It looked like it hadn't been there long."

"Is it being examined for DNA?"

"With the greatest urgency our fine forensics department can manage."

"So, we're stalled. Can I examine the scene more closely?"

"You all are welcome to. I'll introduce you to the officer in charge of the Crime Scene Unit of the Scientific Criminal Investigations Section.

What a mouthful, thought Shona. *I'm suddenly grateful for the Mobile Incident Team Moniker.*

"Colour me all shades of shocked, Miss Shona," said a delightful woman with chocolate eyes and the whitest teeth Shona had ever seen. I never thought we'd have someone Scotch working with us."

Shona, biting her tongue, let the Scotch remark slide despite every Scottish bone in her body wanting to correct it to Scots. She needed this woman on her side.

"It's a pleasure to meet you, Shanice. I was wondering if I could have a look around your crime scene."

"Why, of course, Miss Shona. Y'all are welcome. Maybe Mr Matt here will accompany you and one of my fine officers can accompany your sergeant."

Once the deal was done and the escorts sorted, they headed off along the Wisner Loop Trial. Shona, fit as she was, struggled as, despite it being classed as a medium trail, she was unfamiliar with the terrain and had to be careful where she was treading for both crime scene and conservation reasons. Another thought occurred to her and she recoiled inside. "Are there snakes in the park?

"Not unless you count the ones in our zoo. They have a fine array of Cottonmouth—"

"Too much information. Let's just leave it at I won't step on any, right here, right now, in this park."

Matt's laugh was light relief from the grisly task ahead. "We'll return you to Scotland safe and sound, Miss Shona."

"I'm glad to hear it."

After a through walk around they found nothing. There were footprints aplenty but working out which ones would help them was a forlorn hope - until Shona stood stock still. "Matt," she yelled after his retreating back.

He turned around. "What's with the hollering. You 'bout gave me a conniption fit."

"Did you say to be careful stepping off the trail?"

"Sure did, Ma'am. This here's littered with protected species."

"Well, someone's been trampling around in there." She pointed towards a space surrounded by brush. The brush looked as if it had recently been disturbed. Matt had to bend down to see it.

Matt spoke into a radio. "Can someone from CSU come to..." he gave coordinates and they both waited.

Shanice herself appeared. "Y'all need some help?"

"Has this been logged, Shanice?"

The officer bent down. "Why I don't think it has." She spoke into her radio, listened to the response, and said, "No. Looks a few days old to me."

"I'd agree." Matt wiped sweat from his forehead. "How'd we miss this."

"Don't you go contaminating my crime scene with your sweat now." She scowled at him. "I'd say it needed little Miss Shona here to spot it. The rest of us were way too small."

Shona, at six foot seven, had never been called small before but didn't think this was the time to point it out. It might not even be important.

"I'll take myself a little look," said Shanice. She called on her radio for backup and waited until someone in a white suit lumbered up carrying what looked like an evidence box. He or she, and the second person carrying a camera, was also tall.

They must all be giants in the NOPD was Shona's first thought. She stood back, tapping a staccato rhythm with her foot. All this letting other people take the lead didn't come natural to her but as a guest in a foreign force, she had to take a back seat. So she waited, if not entirely patiently, until Shanice and her compadres reappeared.

"There was a damp patch. Looks like someone, or something, was doing their business in there. It's cooler but humid in there so not entirely dried up." She waved in the direction of white garbed body number one. "Officer Broderick has samples." Then at Body number two. "Officer Jamieson has photos." With that all three disappeared up the trail.

Matt Hernandez unfolded himself from where he had been leaning against a tree. "I think it's time for our visit to the Voodoo Museum.

"Why do we need to visit a museum?" but she was speaking to his retreating back. Nothing different from Dundee she thought.

57

They collected Peter and another patrol car whisked them to Dumaine Street and The New Orleans Historic Voodoo Museum. On the way Matt explained the manager of the museum knew more about voodoo and the current and previous practitioners than anyone else on the planet.

"I'm no' going in there," said Peter, a grim look on his face. "It's against my religion."

"Did you know voodoo has many elements of Catholicism in it," said Matt.

"I don't care. I'm no' going in."

Shona, taking in his flushed complexion said, "It's fine." She pointed to a café across the road. "Go in there and have a cold drink. I'll brief you when we get out."

"Thanks, Ma'am" He loped off before he'd completed the sentence.

"He's a staunch Catholic," explained Shona. "Come on, let's interrogate the manager."

"We don't do much interrogating round here, we're more into chatting." Matt pushed the door open.

"Figure of speech." She followed him in from the bright

sunlight to the dark interior. They stood for a minute until their eyes adjusted. Shona took in the strong scent of incense and musty relics wondering what she had let herself in for.

"Before we meet Mr. Bradley, we'll take a stroll round and let you see what we're dealing with."

"Shona couldn't make head nor tail of anything. It seemed to be a mishmash of different religions and relics, none of which computed in her brain. Shona liked things nice and orderly and orderly this was not. Then she noticed something she did recognise. Relieved, she bent down and took a closer look. "Is that altar for real? Do people really believe all that mumbo—"

"I wouldn't like to say, Ma'am. "The officer wiped his brow with a pristine navy-blue handkerchief that matched his uniform. "Wouldn't want ya'll to take any chances now, would we."

His dark brown eyes stared into Shona's. Unblinking. A shiver ran down her spine.

"Is there anywhere else to visit on this magical mystery tour?"

"Of course, Ma'am. We've a way to go yet. Y'all will get to see most of our fine city."

Shona had a feeling the bits she would get to see wouldn't be that fine. She did have to admit though, the French Quarter was stunning. All that old-fashioned charm, even if it did seem to be mixed with a less charming underbelly.

"Anyways, we've Mr. Bradley to talk to."

Mr Bradley was a wizened pixie of a man with skin like leather and a twinkle in his eyes and an Irish brogue. He handed them each a large bottle of ice-cold water. "Ya'll will be needing this."

"We sure do. I'd like you to meet Detective Inspector Shona McKenzie from Scotland."

"Now, isn't it fine to be meeting a fellow Celt."

"Which part of Ireland are you from?"

"I'm from N'Orleans, Miss Shona. I picked up the brogue from me parents who came over here from County Cork."

Shona guzzled the rest of her water and wiped the drops running down her chin. "Have you got another of these?"

He dug down inside a small cooler and handed two over. "I believe you've some questions you want to be asking."

"Do you know anything about a group called Voodoo For All."

"Young Matt here gave me the heads up you might be asking about that lot, so I prepared."

"Appreciated, thank you."

Some tourists wandered by, and Bradley called to a woman standing in the next room, "You're in charge, I'm going through the back."

"Sure thing."

"Best thing I ever did was marrying a Creole woman. They're the salt of the earth, especially that one." He nodded in the direction of the museum.

Shona, having no clue what creole meant, made a note to look it up the minute she could. She followed the man into a small room even more crowded than the museum, if that were possible. He offered them coffee and for once, Shona declined. All this old-fashioned southern charm and hospitality was delightful, but it was slowing down the investigation. Someone else could get murdered while they exchanged pleasantries. She was still anxious that the murderer would turn their eye to Baby Jesus and the thought of a baby being killed in any manner, never mind such a horrific one, curdled her stomach.

Bradley, or Mr Bradley as Shona now thought of him, gave them a run-down of voodoo from A to Z. Shona was fascinated to hear that voodoo dolls were nothing about hurting people but were originally a way of keeping track of money owed. *Well, I never, how did it go from debt to murder from afar?*

"VFA were a branch of voodoo who wanted to bring it to the

masses. They went out into the streets and talked about it, trying to recruit and convert people. You could say they were the evangelicals of the voodoo world."

"One would assume if they went around murdering people, they are all locked up in your most secure prison." Shona raised one eyebrow in Matt's direction.

"Not at all, Miss Shona. I've investigated them, and they were completely harmless. Not even a sniff of a voodoo doll. They basically wanted to turn voodoo into a major religion."

"I thought it already was fairly major but is it classed as a religion?"

Bradley stepped in again. "It is, one based on ancestral spirits and patron saints. Although they do revere the dead, they don't hasten the living there."

By this point, Shona's head was spinning. Could this get any stranger. "So, have you nay idea who may be doing this?"

"No, but I'm working on it. Let me chat to my contacts and I'll be in touch."

"If you could do that today, Mr Bradley, NOPD would 'preciate it."

"I'm on it, y'all."

"Thank you, Bradley, and I mean that. Your museum is amazing, and I've learned so much about Voodoo and its origins. Who knew it was so fascinating?"

"You're welcome. Ya'll come back and see us, now."

"You bet. I'll be back before I leave N'Orleans.

Shona, sleep deprived and jet lagged, felt like she was on drugs of the psychedelic kind. It was also a long way past breakfast and her blood sugar had plummeted.

"Matt, taking in her white face, said, "Let's go to Café Beignet for coffee and beignets."

Shona, who'd heard about the sugar laden pastries, liked the sound of this plan and was prepared to tuck in. She was not prepared for was Bourbon Street where the café was located.

Bourbon street was historic, loud, and jammed with tourists. Both Shona and Peter's faces were a picture."

"Yon lassie's no' got a top on."

"Peter, speak English." Shona had clocked the puzzled look on Matt's face.

"Why isn't she wearing anything on her top half. Are you going to arrest her?"

Matt laughed. "It's perfectly legal as her top half is painted."

"What?" even Shona was puzzled now."

"During Mardi Gras there's a tradition of women flashing their breasts for beads. Some women now do it for tourists and ask for tips. There's a law saying you can't wander around with your breasts exposed but if they are painted then they are classed as clothed."

Shona, knowing Peter too well, flashed him a don't even think about it look. The last thing they needed was his unfiltered comments upsetting the local population. New Orleans laws were nothing to do with them. They had enough on their plate with Scottish law, which really was a law unto itself.

Over the beignets, which were as heavenly as they were

made out to be, they updated Peter on the conversation. He broke out in a sweat but merely wiped his brow with a handkerchief and let them talk.

"Where's this taking us," he asked.

"It's taking us to St Louis Cemetery Number 1 and the tomb of Marie Laveau." He stood up as his phone pinged. "Our car is outside right now."

Shona wasn't sure how that would help but followed anyway. Much as she loved seeing the sites, tourism wasn't getting them anywhere. However, once in the car, Matt explained that messages were often left on the tomb, despite it not being allowed. In this case they were keeping a close eye in case a pertinent message was left and had left strict instructions for the messages to remain untouched.

This city is mad but marvellous. Her thoughts were interrupted by the shrill ringing of her phone. Not expecting it, she jumped and her heart beat faster. If this was Douglas, she'd kill him.

Much to Shona's surprise it was Valerie Dickenson. "Shona, I've got a name for you. A Lola Lister was thrown out of VFA for being too extreme. A previous leader of the organisation said she was a right bampot."

If Shona had been in the room with Valerie, she would have hugged her. "You are a total rock star. When I get back on Caledonian soil, I'll take you out to dinner."

"I'll expect it."

She pressed end call, immediately followed by speed dial 6. Roy answered within three rings. "Yo. What's up boss?"

"Yo? You're in Dundee not the states. I need you to do something for me."

"You do realise it's almost 9 pm. I'm at home with a glass of wine."

Blast. "Sorry, I'd forgotten about the time difference. Could you do me a favour. Grab a taxi at the firm's expense, go into the office and do a search on a woman called Lola Lister."

"Sure thing. Although with a name like that I'll probably find her at Cat's Eyes. As an exotic dancer. " He sang the first few lines of a well-known Barry Manilow song about a girl called Lola.

"Don't give up the day job, Roy." In all fairness he wasn't that bad and would go down well when the karaoke machine made an appearance at the Police Scotland Christmas Party. If they ever got to the office Christmas Party. They might be joining NOPD for theirs at this rate.

Hanging up, Shona updated the men and Matt said he'd get a search done his end.

"It might tie in." He made a similar call.

Shona felt better now there was something happening, and a shiver of excitement darted down her spine at the thought of visiting the cemetery. She took in the impressive tombs as Matt led her to the exact grave where the voodoo queen lay. It was, indeed, covered in messages like literary graffiti. Shona and Peter idly looked at them. Matt studied them intently. The graffiti mostly consisted of crosses but with about twenty handwritten messages, some short some rambling. All giving praise to Marie Laveau.

"There's a new one," said Matt. He snapped a picture and messaged it to his team with instructions to do some forensic code analysis on it.

The message read:

'All hail to the Voodoo Queen, the ruler of the universe. Her message resonates throughout the world, from New Orleans to the bayou, and all corners of the world. Today is your day and TOMORROW will be your day. We, in the bayou worship you.'

"What does that mean," asked Peter.

Shona was about to ask the very same question.

"No idea. Maybe nothing but another avid follower talking a load of garbage."

Shona was inclined to go with the fruitcake theory of

someone being a bit overenthusiastic. However, she'd been in the game long enough to realise that it could also bear fruit. Leave no stone, or graffitied tomb, left unturned.

The remainder of the day passed in an endless whirl of discussions and visiting relevant spots. It ended with a Jazz Dinner River Cruise in a paddleboat with Matt's wife and four children. He assured them they could still be called in the middle of the Mississippi and a police speedboat would be sent to rescue them if they were needed urgently. Shona and Peter settled back to enjoy themselves. She tucked in to the main course of Dirty Rice and enjoyed every mouthful but couldn't help noticing Peter's face and the way he shoved the food around his plate with a fork. He was more a fish and chips sort of guy and if it wasn't served in a restaurant or takeaway in Dundee, it wasn't worth bothering about. Still, this sort of thing didn't come along every day and Shona, for one, was going to make the most of every sublimely, relaxing, minute, and did so until she stumbled off the boat clutching a Vieux Carré Cocktail in a go cup, New Orleans style.

She wasn't quite so relaxed when awoken by the harsh sounds of her phone at 3.37 am. "What the…" She fumbled around for the light switch and her phone.

"It's the middle of the night." She also had an entire jazz band performing a concert in her head if her headache were anything to go by. She was beginning to regret that last cocktail and resolved to find out exactly what was in a Vieux Carré. She would wager nothing healthy whatsoever with the exception of the decorative cherries.

Sorry, Ma'am. We've been in for hours." Roy sounded far too cheery for her liking. In fact, he didn't sound sorry at all.

"Is this you getting your own back for me sending you into work last night? If so, I swear—"

"Not at all, Ma'am. Would I dare. I've some info for you."

She sat up and rubbed her eyes. "Spit it out."

"Lola Lister isn't a pole dancer. She, according to her online presence, is the most boring person in the world. However, she has shared posts relating to witches, covens, and curses."

Shona sat up higher, all tiredness forgotten. "Interesting. Anything else."

"I saved the best for last. She's related to the grannie of that wee boy we interviewed."

Shona's brain exploded as she took in this new information. "You keep digging. Send Nina and Jason round to Rena Germaine's house and find out where we can get hold of Lola."

Shona's mind whirred with all the permutations of what this could mean. Did the gran know anything? Did the aunt? "Also, send Abigail and Iain to interview Joshua's aunt. Although I don't see how that indolent bag of bones could stir herself enough to listen to anyone."

She leapt from her bed and wondered if she should ring Matt. Deciding it could wait until she had more information, she made a coffee and clambered into bed. Sometime later she fell into a fitful doze.

Two hours later she was wide awake and tucking into a cheese, pepper, and mushroom omelette. She'd heard nothing more from the team and decided to wait until she had more information before briefing Matt. It could pan out to nothing, although every sensitive fibre in Shona's body was telling her otherwise.

Today they walked to the station and on arriving donned stab vests and guns once more. Thankfully, no one had insisted they carry them when they were off duty – yet.

As the current plan seemed to be waiting for information to come back, Shona briefed the American team on what she'd heard overnight. Then she attempted to put her jumbled thoughts into some semblance of order but failed miserably. Then, it hit her. The indolent aunt could be both the witch and their killer.

"Can I see the piece of black cloth you found at the crime scene?"

"We'd be happy to oblige, Ma'am, but do you mind telling us why?" Matt was as polite as always, but Shona had the feeling he thought she was half baked. She explained about the woman dressed in black and the witch at the crime scene.

Matt sent an officer scurrying to the evidence room, telling him to make it quick.

They filled the time in pouring more coffee and eating some cakes that had miraculously appeared. "Not doughnuts then?" asked Peter.

"American cops and donuts are an urban myth. At one point only donut shops were open in the middle of the night and cops grabbed coffee there." His dazzling smile appeared. "Although, I may have eaten a few in my younger days."

Shona bit into a slice of something she couldn't quite name. Despite this it tasted delicious and hit the spot.

It seemed like a lifetime until the cop whizzed through the door clutching an evidence bag and a brace of official looking forms. "Got it, but you've to sign these, Captain." He hurled the forms at Matt, who signed them with a NOPD pen. He rifled around in a drawer and pulled out some more pens. "Here," he handed them over to Shona and Peter.

Shona was more interested in the contents of the evidence bag.

Seeing the longing look on her face, he shoved it across the desk to her. "I'm not sure what you'll get from it at the moment, but any enlightenment would be warmly accepted."

Shona studies the scrap of fabric closely. "Are we allowed to take it out?"

"I'm afraid not, Miss Shona. Too high a risk of contamination."

"Any chance of picking up DNA from it?"

"Done already. No known match to anyone in our database."

"I've a theory. I'm going to ring my department, see what

they've dragged up already, and ask them to do a DNA sample their end."

"What's on your mind?"

"Let me make the call and I'll update you the minute it's over. Is there somewhere quiet I can go?"

She was deposited in a utilitarian room with the minimum of furniture. Shona's feeling was that all police stations, wherever you went in the world, resembled the gulags. They'd left her with a gargantuan mug of coffee that would take a weightlifter to pick up. She took a sip and dialled Nina's number, thanking every star above that Police Scotland had ponied up for international calling before she left.

"Hey, Shona, how's it going out there in the sun."

"Couldn't be better. Good grief woman, I'm not here on holiday. What's the skinny from the interviews?"

"Good news and bad news. Good news first. Rena confirmed that Lola is her great cousin twice removed. Some sort of family hanger on. They're not close but she's always up for babysitting and has been hanging around a lot since the kids lost their mother."

"What's her take on her?"

"A bit weird. Doesn't talk much. Spends all her time at the council gyms, working out."

"What's she's training for?"

"I went to the gym and flashed my—"

"I'm sure you did. I'm just as sure it worked."

"My ID card."

"Yeh, right."

The laughter coming through the earpiece gave Shona a sense of normality. She almost wished her friend was there with her.

"According to the guys at the gym she does a lot of strength training, especially weightlifting. Apparently, she was training for competitions. Roy's looking into it."

"Brilliant. She's the top of my suspect list. How did the interview with her go? Did anyone bring her in for questioning?"

"No interview. No questioning? The bad news is, she's flown the coop."

"I'd bet a year's salary on the fact she's flown on a British Airways plane to New Orleans."

"Yep. Abigail's on it."

"Get a warrant and search her house from top to bottom. First task, get something with DNA and get it analysed yesterday. Top priority. Straight to the front of the queue. Results to be emailed to me immediately."

"On it."

B ack in the main room, Shona briefed them and explained why she was so interested in the piece of cloth. "I think Lola Lister is our killer. I also think she's in New Orleans."

Matt sprang into action, directing his team to carry out different tasks. Internet searches, airline searches, chasing up the DNA, checking park employee records etc. With a flurry of movement, they all disappeared taking Peter with them. This left Matt and Shona to update the boards and tap their fingers. Ten minutes in, Matt said, "Come on. I'm taking you to the crime lab to see if the soil samples from Audobon Park came up with DNA. We'll encourage them to push it through."

The crime lab was on Lakeside Road, housed in an impressive building that Dundee would kill for. It was part of the university. "Is this for the whole state?"

"No, just one of our smaller crime labs. Our great state has ten in total."

Good God in heaven is everything in America bigger and better.

They were slammed but listened to Matt, agreed as to the urgency of the situation, and said they'd look and see where they were with it. They left Matt's phone number and retired across the road to drink yet more coffee. This was worse than Dundee. At least there she could bark orders or visit people. Here, she was at the mercy of others.

Thirty-seven minutes later – Shona counted every frustratingly slow one of them – Matt's phone rang. "We're on our way."

They left the crime lab with a copy of the DNA profile and a letter that said the two samples were a hundred percent match.

"We just need to wait for the DNA to come through from our end. This is excruciating."

"There are other words I could use but I'll abstain in the presence of a lady."

There were two NOPD baseball caps sitting on Matt's desk when they returned. He handed one to Shona. "Present for you. The other one is for your sergeant. It will keep the heat off."

Shona thanked him and plonked it on her head.

"You might want to put your ponytail between through the gap at the back. It will be more comfortable."

She adjusted it thinking life was so much easier at home where you just worried about clothes and waterproofs. Then she felt guilty at the thought of home as she hadn't rung Douglas since she arrived. "I've got to make a quick call. Update for the procurator fiscal." She omitted the fact the PF was also her fiancé.

Douglas was fine, as were the children. They all missed her, especially Alice who wondered if she'd make it home for the school play. "I doubt it." She updated him on the current situation and asked him to brief the Chief Inspector.

"I'm sure Thomas will be delighted to hear from you."

"I'm sure he will." Shona wasn't so sure the Chief was missing her that much. His life was probably much quieter without her underfoot. Hers was certainly much quieter as not one person had told her off since she got here. Unless you counted the voodoo warning.

An hour and three mugs of coffee later, all hell let loose, or so it seemed. Everyone returned, all trying to give their feedback at once.

"Lola Lister flew into the country a week ago – JFK then Louis Armstrong International." Shona had no idea who he was but given his demeanour decided to call him Officer Perky.

"What's the address on her landing card?" Matt had a gleam of hope in his eyes.

"Didn't need it. Apparently, she's got dual citizenship."

"She's not got even a hint of an American accent. Any idea why she's got dual citizenship?" Shona couldn't quite get her head around all of this. At least in Dundee everyone was related to or knew everyone else.

"I'm looking into it." Perky trotted off to continue his task and the door slammed behind him.

Shona winced. "Why isn't there more information on her. I thought you could trace everyone in the USA."

"We can, Miss Shona, but sometimes patience is needed." Matt smiled which took the admonishment from his words. They were implied anyway.

Shona was in short supply of patience. However, in deference to the team currently in charge, she kept her counsel. At least she wasn't being threatened with dismissal. Maybe the chief's 'get this solved now 'attitude was rubbing off on her. She rubbed her arms; the air conditioning was cold enough to freeze the bayou. She wondered if she'd ever get to see the bayou. "I'm taking my coffee outside for five minutes while I make a phone call.

"It's a pleasant day. Ma'am. You'll enjoy it out there." Officer Perky's mate, who Shona vaguely remembered was called Dobbs, held the door open for her.

She leaned against the wall, took a large swig of coffee and rang Nina again. "Any updates?"

"The DNA analysis is winging it's way to us in about five minutes. I'll send it straight on."

"Anything else of import?"

"We canvassed Lola's neighbours and colleagues. They all say she's completely of her rocker."

"What about her friends?"

"Doesn't have any."

"Relatives?"

"No one but Rema is owning up to her."

"I'd better go back in. Keep your phone handy in case I need you."

They were back in hurry up and wait mode until another young officer blew through the door like a hurricane.

"Slow down, Cormier. This is a police station not a baseball field."

"Sorry, Captain." He screeched to a halt at Matt's feet and then looked from him to Shona. "We're growing old, Cormier. Are you going to tell us?" Matt was in full on, in charge captain mode.

"As instructed, I went to speak to the Audobon Park HR department." He stopped and took several deep breaths, the run to get her having knocked the wind out of him.

"And?" Shona couldn't help herself.

"There's no Lola Lister there but there is a Lennie Lister."

"Well done, Officer Cormier. Now, find out if there's any relation between them or if it's merely coincidence."

Cormier bounded off and Matt shouted after him. "Get his address."

"Is there anything I can dae, Ma'am?"

"Call Nina or Abigail. Ask them to find out from Rena Germaine if Lola has any relatives in New Orleans."

Shona dared not hope they were close to closing the case and arresting a killer.

A couple of minutes later, Shona's phone pinged telling her she had an email. It was the DNA Analysis. "Matt, I'm emailing you Lola's DNA. Can you get the crime lab to compare it?"

"On it."

Shona pressed forward on the email, and she assumed Matt did the same. They were getting closer to solving this, she could feel it.

"I can't believe I sat in the same room as our supposed killer and didn't realise it."

"What?" said Matt. "How?"

She explained that Lola had been in an interview with her nephew. Then she thought of something else. "Hang on." She sent a text to Nina: did you find anything in the Lister house that looked like a witch's cloak?

Two minutes later she had her answer: yep. Amongst many other costumes.

She turned to Matt. "I definitely think Lola is our killer."

"All we have to do is find Miss Lola."

And we are going to do that, how?

"That's a very good question, Miss Shona, but you can believe, we gonna do exactly that. Aint no killer ever escaped my clutches and it aint gonna happen now."

Shona had her suspicions he was putting on an exaggerated accent to cover up the fact he had about as much clue as she did.

Ten minutes later Shona's phone rang and when she hung up, she said, "Lennie Lister is Lola's twin. Separated at two years old. He stayed with the father; she returned to Scotland with the mother."

"Let's find out where he lives. If I was a betting man, I'd say she's either using his place as a base or, more likely, they're in cahoots." Matt leapt up. 'We're going to catch ourselves some killers."

"Have we got the address yet?'

"No, but my fine Officers will provide it to us any time now. NOPD, like The Mounties, always get their man."

"Or woman," added Shona.

"Dinnae be leaving the women oot."

Mat raised a quizzical eyebrow.

"English, Peter."

They were deflected from Peter's mangling of the English language because, as if by magic, Officer Dobbs hand delivered a sheet of paper containing the address. The search was a go.

"Do we need a warrant?" asked Shona, not sure of the proper protocol. The only thing she knew about the American Police she gleaned from telly programmes.

"Officer Dobbs will be applying for one as we speak. By the time we're ready to go we'll have a warrant in our hands." He chewed on his bottom lip before adding, "This is going to be more difficult than we thought. By the looks of the address, this house is deep in the bayou."

"What's the bayou," asked Peter.

"No time to explain, you'll find out soon enough." He bolted towards the door, all restless efficiency and pent-up energy. His team followed suit.

Shona and Peter headed after them - it was time to show America what Scotland was made of. Although Shona couldn't help but wonder what they were letting themselves in for.

Peter leaned in close to her ear. "What's the bayou?"

"Swamps."

"Swamps? I cannae do swamps. The mosquitoes will eat me alive."

"Suck it up, sunshine and stop your whining. Most of the team would kill to be in your place."

"Maybe no' the best phrase to use under the circumstances, Ma'am."

Shona was too busy trying to keep up with Matt to answer or care.

62

Getting ready to arrest someone in the USA meant a lot of gear to be donned. Shona balked at being issued with rifles. "No. We've no clue how to use them and, given we've no clue how to navigate in the bayou, we'd be a liability."

"You might need them. If not for our suspects, then for the alligators."

"Alligators. I'm no' going anywhere where there's alligators."

"Peter, for heaven's sake, you're giving Scotland a bad name."

"Y'all will be safe with us. We grew up with alligators."

"There probably aren't that many anyway." Peter's voice held a tinge of hope.

"About two million but they're spread about." Matt made sure their stab vests were on securely and then did the same with the holsters. "Check your pistols."

Peter had a look that said he was going to refuse to go but a look from Shona stopped him.

"Right, are we all ready? On the minibus. Go"

. . .

The minute they stepped off the bus, Peter began to sweat. Whether from heat, humidity, or fear, even he couldn't tell.

Within minutes Shona was trying to pull the NOPD t-shirt from her body where it clung like a new-born on the nipple. The humidity made it difficult to breathe and the stench of wet and rotting vegetation hung in the air, slapping her in the face at every step. This was going to be punishingly hard. Her lungs protested as she forced air in and out. Maybe it wasn't such a good idea to bring Peter. All she needed was him having another heart attack in the middle of the bayou. Now she was worried about Peter and alligators. Her heart was beating like the entire band of the pipes and drums was inside her chest.

Matt was barking out orders like the sergeant major of the aforementioned band. His officers jumped to it immediately: no arguments, no murmur of dissent, no grim looks. Each one knew his place and carried out their task efficiently and with the utmost professionalism. Shona was impressed and wondered if she could swap them for her lot. Then she decided she'd miss the camaraderie.

Matt turned to Shona and Peter. "Y'all need to follow us closely and listen for commands. If I raise my hand, you stop. If I wave you forward, you move again."

Shona had a sudden urge to say, "Aye, aye, Captain," but, realising the importance of the message, kept her mouth shut. It really could be a matter of life and death.

A radio crackled into life. Matt pressed a button saying, "Hernandez."

"Roger that. Thanks." More crackling. "Will do. Thanks."

Shona looked at him with question marks in both eyes.

"Your Lola's DNA matches the DNA in the park. Or at least some of it does. There's some closely matched DNA which we are betting is Lennie's."

Shona punched the air. "So, we're on the right track?"

"Looks like it. There was also sperm found, again DNA analysis of which would suggest it is Lennie's."

"TMI." Shona screwed her face up.

Peter had a look of someone who'd heard it all before.

"They also said take care as the alligators come out at dusk."

Shona swallowed. Peter uttered nothing more than a whining sound. Neither were sure which was worse – their killers or the wildlife.

They set off briskly, a pace Shona wasn't sure either she or Peter could keep up, despite the fact they both exercised regularly - she running and he walking. This was something else again in heat so cloying it cleaved the soul. Exposed tree branches were a death trap to the unwary and in the encroaching dusk, with only headlamps for light, were doubly so. At least there was no water. Then a thought shot through Shona's head. "How far from the water can alligators travel?"

"I'm not real sure, Ma'am, but they can reach speeds of thirty-five miles per hour on land," said a young cop in too cheerful a manner for Shona's liking.

Matt chipped in, "They can also leap up to eight feet in the air."

"Okay, we've heard enough."

Matt's laugh rang out into the still air, startling a beautiful red winged bird, who shot screeching into the sky. "Don't worry, the alligator eating turtles will stop them before they get to you."

"Are you having a laugh?"

"No, Miss Shona. I would never lie to you."

Good God in heaven; to what sort of weird and wonderful land had the firm sent her. As they moved deeper into the bayou, the vegetation grew thicker and the trees more towering and closer together. Now at the swamp proper, brackish water gave out a scent that burned the nostrils and clung to the clothes. Shona wanted to take shallow breaths. She forced herself to take deep ones. She forced herself to keep putting one foot in front of the other, despite everything in her body screaming at her to run back to safety. She was never going to complain about Dundee again. Worrying about alligators had never previously been a problem but the thought of meeting one 'up close and personal' had her heart pounding and her fight or flight response on high alert.

Shona scratched feverishly at her arms. Despite covering herself in half a can of mosquito repellent, which was more likely to kill her than an alligator, the evil little suckers were still eating her alive. She decided the Louisiana Bayou was the most beautiful hellhole on earth.

After what seemed like hours, but was probably less than an hour, Matt indicated for them to stop. A wooden house, set back from the swamp but still up on stilts, lay about 600 yards ahead.

"Shona stood stock still and whispered, "Is this it?" She didn't know her heart could beat any faster, but it managed it despite physiology indicating otherwise.

"No. We're going to ask them where the Listers live."

"Sorry?"

"It's the only way you'll find anyone in hundreds of miles of swampland. You come with me."

Matt knocked on a rickety front door, pushed it open, and stepped inside. Shona thought that was a bit forward of him, but she was willing to admit she didn't know the local customs. She stood on the doorstep until he indicated she should follow. The interior was gloomy, cramped, and lit by candles. The heat factor trebled. Shona wiped her brow and prayed her DNA wasn't contaminating anything.

"What y'all want boy? Who dis wit you?" The strong voice came from a woman who looked to be about 183 years of age.

Shona wasn't sure if she was mixed race, or her leathery skin was tanned from years of the Louisiana sun. Either way, her voice didn't quite add up to her supposed age.

Shona figured out she was asking who she was. Matt introduced her and said she was a Scottish policeman."

"Y'all Scotch are welcome to Mama Mathilde's house."

Good grief, the Lister's could slaughter the entire cast of the nativity while all these southern pleasantries were being played out. She kept schtum. When in Rome and all that.

"We're looking for a girl called Lola Lister. Do you know them?"

"Why you looking for her your own self?"

Shona wasn't sure where this was going, Was the woman going to protect a fellow swamp resident.

"She's a suspect in a murder. Several murders, Auntie."

"Dat girl is couyon. Her brother too. Dem one couyon family. Dat don't surprise me none she done gone and murdered someone."

Shona, eyebrows raised, turned to Matt.

"That girl is crazy and so is her brother. They're a crazy family. Cajun English."

Good grief thought Shona. *Not only do I need to worry about Scottish but now Cajun as well.*

"Where will we find her?" asked Matt.

"Deep down in the bayou. Past old Mama Benoit's place. Dey has a home dere."

"Thank you," said Shona.

Matt followed up with, "Byen Mersi." Shona looked at him again. "More Cajun. Cajun French"

Once outside, Shona asked, "Is she really your auntie?"

"She surely is, Miss Shona. I'm half creole, half Hispanic."

That explained his sizzling good looks and the sex god like aura he exuded thought Shona. *Thank goodness he's married as I'd be tempted to dally.*

"So, what's the updated plan?" Shona pulled at her stab vest in an attempt to let some air in. She could almost feel the water pouring off her t-shirt. There was heat and there was this. Still, she wouldn't let Scotland down and was ready to do whatever it took to bring a killer to justice. On the bright side, at least it wasn't snowing.

"The plan is to continue deep into the bayou and ask Mama Benoit if she knows anything that will help us."

Time seemed to crawl and yet every minute meant there was a still a brace of killers on the loose.

"Are we actually going to catch this pair," asked Peter. "If they scarper into this godforsaken wilderness, we'll never find them."

"Good point." She hurried up to Matt and said, "What if they flee?"

"Bayou folks know the bayou as intimately as they know their own bodies." He stared at her, unblinking. "We'd be in big trouble."

A shiver ran down Shona's spine. "What about you? Do you have an intimate knowledge of the bayou."

"More of a passing glance than intimacy."

"So, we're stuffed."

"Not at all, Miss Shona. NOPD never fails.'

"Good to know."

63

Their brisk walk continued as darkness fell and they travelled deeper into the bayou. Shona and Peter kept close to their American colleagues, sure they'd come to a sticky end if they moved to the left or the right.

Alligator eyes glinted in the torchlight. Shona moved closer to Matt's back thinking it might get him first if it decided to attack.

Eventually, Matt stopped them again and he disappeared inside another house taking Shona with him."

"What y'all want wit dem. Dem bad people. Bad, bad people."

"We know, Mama. That's why we need to arrest them and take them out of the bayou.

"Dose devil people. Bring evil to dis bayou. Dem live up-river. Turn left at the old cypress, walk 'bout 500 yards. Dere their shack will be."

"Do you know anything about them."

"Couyon. Dere daddy was couyon. Dem mama was well out of dis."

"Which way Couyon?"

"Dem hate us people who follow the Lord. Dem devils."

"What about Christmas."

Dey worse at dem times. Christmas and Easter."

Shona and Matt exchanged looks, Shona's slightly puzzled.

"Thanks' Mama."

Once outside he asked, "Did you understand that?"

"Just about. I take it Christmas and Easter are a big problem for Lola and Lennie."

"And their daddy. Or was. He's in a cemetery somewhere."

"Do we know where we're going?"

"We surely do. Time to catch us some killers."

Shona was sceptical that they'd ever find anyone, never mind Lola and Lennie, but she was willing to give Matt the benefit of the doubt. If she were strictly honest, she didn't have a choice.

As they drew closer, Matt stopped them.

"Come in close." He whispered, indicating a circle round his body.

Everyone took several steps forward until they were in a tight huddle.

"Dobbs, you're with Sergeant Johnston. Take the back."

Dobbs nodded.

"Fontenot and Theriot, you're giving us cover. Detective Inspector McKenzie and I will take the front."

"Yes, Sir."

Captain Hernandez carried on giving out instructions, obviously used to being in charge. Shona was impressed by his handling of the situation and his calm demeanour. They were told to maintain silence and dim their headlamps. They set off once more, their steps slow, each one carefully placed to minimise noise. Yard by painful yard, they moved towards their goal, senses on high alert and adrenaline surging through their bodies. The American officers cradled their rifles, ready for action. Even Shona and Peter had their hands on their guns.

Then, as they crept towards the cabin, a scream echoed

through the bayou. Birds, disturbed from their slumbers, took flight uttering raucous cries.

In the midst of the commotion Shona saw Officer Fontenot lying on the ground, clutching his leg. Matt switched up the brightness on his headlamp.

"Are you bleeding?" Matt barked out his voice urgent.

"I don't think so." The officer looked closer. "No breaks in my pants."

"Alligators can smell blood from more distance than you'd ever imagine and also 1ml in ten gallons of water," Matt explained to the Scots.

Peter moaned and Shona felt like joining him.

The crack of a shotgun rang out. Each of them pressed closer to the trees.

"Fontenot, can you walk."

The officer stood up warily and tried it out. He made sure he was still hugging the tree. "Yes Sir."

"Right, it's a go. Headlamps on. Cover."

Fontenot and Theriot instantly took position and started firing towards a ramshackle hut situated in a small clearing. The smell of rotting garbage rose above the wet bayou smell. Shona felt like gagging. The hulks of rotting boats were littered about the place

"Move."

The rest of them raced from tree to tree until they were at the edge of the clearing. "Dobbs led Peter around the back, while Matt started firing towards the one open window. They could hear shots around the back of the hut and Shona started praying hard they were coming from Dobbs and Peter rather than aimed at them. Shona could hear Peter muttering a Hail Mary, or at least she was hoping that's what it was. They needed all the help they could get. Shadows danced on the edges of the light from their headlamps. Matt pointed into the darkness and waived forward; Dobbs peeled off, Peter following. Darkness swallowed their carefully fleeing figures. Minutes later gunfire was heard from the trees behind the huts.

At the sound the shadow in the window disappeared Then, more gunshots rang out into the night.

Shona shoved aside the cold ring of fear which clutched at her chest. Fear, not for herself but her sergeant. Instead, she focussed on what lay ahead. Focussed on Matt and any instructions he might give, watching his every move her senses on high alert. He shut off his headlamp and Shona followed suit. Then he waved her forward and pointed to a rotting hull in the middle of the clearing. She darted towards it and threw herself behind it, thankful the safety catch was firmly on her pistol. No shooting herself in the foot. No injuries. No blood. She shuddered, detached herself from her feelings, and peered over the decaying wood. A strong smell of mould assaulted her nostrils, but adrenaline overpowered the stench blotting it from her brain. Matt lay close beside her, so close she could smell a faint hint of aftershave mingled with the musky scent of sweat. She moved in closer and whispered into his ear, "What's our next move?"

He leaned into her and whispered back, "That, Ma'am, depends on how many guns and how much ammunition these hometown boys have."

"Any chance of backup?"

"I don't want them to focus on the front. I'd say they're focussing all their efforts on the back right now."

Shona turned around, leaned against the hull, and took a few deep breaths. She felt the wood shift and sat upright again before turning and peering over the hull once more.

"If we move to that hull..." she pointed about a hundred yards ahead, "We'd be closer."

"Let's go," he muttered, the sound of his voice barely breaking the stillness as it evaporated into the absorbing blanket of heat and humidity.

They scuttled across and took cover once again.

"It's quiet," said Shona. "Too quiet."

"Yes, Ma'am. That worries me."

Blimey, son, you're in charge. Don't go getting all worried on me. I need you to be certain sure.

6 4

S he was almost at the stage of mentally writing his obituary when she noticed a shadow in her peripheral vision. She stiffened. With a barely noticeable flick of her elbow, she nudged Matt gently in the side and pointed to her right.

"Someone's fleeing." He leapt to his feet and hollered on the others; all thoughts of silence thrown to the non-existent wind this was not the time for caution. "Quick, they've got the advantage of knowing this here bayou, inside out."

They switched their lights on and bolted off in hot pursuit adrenaline pumping in full-on action mode.

The crack of a pistol alerted them to the ongoing danger. No one stopped. Hearts pumping overtime they kept running. The danger of their surrounding terrain did not escape Shona. She didn't care. One step. Another. And another. Foliage tugged at her ankles, sharp edges penetrated her trousers and ripped her skin. She didn't care. Stumbling over tree roots and vegetation she didn't even know existed, she kept her eye on the prize. Capturing her killer. This was personal. The relatives of her victims deserved justice; the people of Dundee deserved answers.

At the point of wondering how long they could keep this breakneck speed up, a scream reverberated into the night. Matt headed towards it, then stopped dead. Shona smacked into him, and he steadied them both. The others screeched to a halt beside them.

Shona's brain turned the scene before her into a slow-motion movie. Lennie's leg was clutched between the powerful jaws of an enormous alligator. The alligator moved backwards at a speed Shona didn't know was possible and the man disappeared below the water. She heard Peter say, "Jesus, Mary and Joseph, and she knew he was crossing himself.

Lola's screams shattered their immobility and the officers reached for guns.

"No. Help him. Get him." She turned towards them and had taken no more than one step, when in a blur of motion another alligator appeared. Urgent shrieks rang out as the alligator grabbed her. They watched as the woman's leg was torn in two. Matt, taking aim, fired once and shot the beast between the eyes. Shona made a move towards the woman to drag her away, but Matt stopped her.

"Not with that much blood around."

Before Shona could work out why another alligator appeared, and Lola joined her brother in the murky waters of the swamp.

65

Shona, never at a loss for words, couldn't formulate one single one. She stood, shaking. Then, she doubled over and deposited her lunch over the swamp in front of her. The rancid smell of vomit joined that of stagnant creek water and rotting vegetation. It wasn't pleasant.

Matt handed her some water. "Swallow this. Come on, we need to get out of here."

He grabbed her arm and pulled her away from the water as they retreated at a punishing pace all the way back to Mama Benoit's place.

Once she felt safe, Shona turned to Peter. His face was grey. "Are you okay?"

He looked at her for a few minutes before saying, "That was horrific. I'll never forget it."

"It's going to be burned on my brain for life as well." She didn't like the look of Peter. "Hold up just now and we'll get you checked by a doctor."

Mama handed them each a concoction that looked revolting with a smell that punched at the nostrils and sped all the way up to the brain."

"I'm no' drinking that."

Shona threw him a look that said he'd better or there would be trouble.

"It will do y'all good. Dis is my most potent cure. Ya'll drink it your own self."

Shona took a deep breath, gulped it down, and started coughing. Peter did the same. A few minutes later Shona said, "That stuff's amazing. What's in it."

"Mama don't tell non-one what's in her medicines."

"You need to bottle that and sell it all around the world. You'd be a millionaire," said Peter.

"Dis Mama got everything she need right here in the dis bayou."

And alligators, thought Shona, but she kept her council. Mama had managed to reach a ripe old age living amongst the creatures of the swamp so she must know a thing or two about the local wildlife. Who was she to tell her how to live safely far away from alligators and swamps? She looked around her. This home was comfortable and colourful with sofas and chairs covered by bright blankets.

Whilst Shona and Peter were recovering from shock, Matt had radioed through to the station, and they were sending out the relevant authorities to try and recover the bodies. "We've to wait here until they arrive."

Peter stretched his legs. His colour had improved somewhat but Shona still wanted him seen by a doctor when they got back to New Orleans. She thought longingly of the bright lights of the city far away from alligators, drownings, and mosquitos. A shiver ran down her spine when she thought about the way the twins had met their grisly end. She wouldn't wish that on anyone.

As if he had read her mind, Matt said, "No one deserves to die in the jaws of an alligator." He stopped and stared at her, unblinking. "No matter what they've done."

"Couldn't agree more."

Silence fell and they all sank inside their own thoughts as the gruesome scene played out like a horror movie on their eyelids. No one uttered another word until reinforcements came banging at the door. They burst through it all high energy, enthusiasm, and loud voices. Mama dispensed drinks, and Matt outlined what had happened. He said he would show them exactly where it was.

"I'll accompany you," said Shona, swallowing as bile rose in her throat.

"Are you sure?'

"Yes." She turned to Peter. "You stay here."

"Aye, I'm no' wanting tae go back there anyhow."

Shona headed towards the creek wondering whether Scots or Cajun was more difficult to get your head around.

The creek looked peaceful; not one alligator disturbed the tranquillity. Moonlight filtered through and lit the water. Nature at its stunning best despite the cruel underbelly. She was glad she returned as she could think of this picture rather than the one of death and terror. The feeling of dread slipped from her, and she straightened her shoulders.

66

In the bus back to the city, Shona said under her voice, "Matt, I want Peter seen by a doctor." She explained about his heart attack and added, "I'd feel happier if the medics said he was good to go. We don't want another corpse on our hands." Also, the chief would sack her on the spot if she went home without him.

Matt nodded and dropped them off at the hospital. "Give me a call when you're finished, and I'll get someone to pick y'all up."

They entered the hospital which was bright, airy, and all high ceilings and plate glass windows.

"You're making a right show of me, dragging me here. There's nothing wrong wi' me."

"We'll let the doctor decide that. I don't want to have to explain to the long-suffering Mrs Johnston why she's missing her husband - during her favourite time of the year."

That effectively shut him up. Shona waited with him until he was called through. The doctor assured her he was in good hands and that she might as well find herself a drink as the tests could take a couple of hours. She was out the door almost before he could finish the sentence, leaving Peter to it having told him to ring her the minute he heard anything.

Settling into a comfortable chair in a coffee shop in the foyer she inhaled the aroma of freshly brewed coffee. It shot to her brain like an explosion of adrenaline and settled her jangling nerves. The first ambrosial sip danced on her taste buds and slipped down to her stomach with the ease of an old friend. Her thoughts turned to the case and how on earth she was going to tell the chief this one. She needed to ring him but not in the middle of a café. Even Louisianians, used to the vagaries of the bayous, might lose the contents of their stomachs at the tale she would have to tell. She took another sip of coffee and thought back to the interview with Joshua. Was there anything in his aunt's demeanour that should have alerted her to the fact she was a serial killer. Did she miss anything. She shivered, whether from the air conditioning or the thought of people dying because she'd missed something, she wasn't quite sure.

She cradled her mug in her hands enjoying the feeling of warmth and letting it soothe her. Her limbs ached and she was sure they'd be able to play dot-to-dot with her mosquito bites. She thought back to the shootout/chase and, again, wondered if there was anything they could have done differently. Something that would have ended in capture rather than death.

Wanting to concentrate on something other than death by alligator she pulled her phone out and called Roy.

"Hey, Ma'am, how's New Orleans? Having fun? Caught our killer yet."

His cheery voice reminded her that 4,410 miles away life went on as normal. A life where people hadn't been changed forever by deaths so horrific the thought of them shredded the brain. "Sort of. Can't talk now. Did you get any info on Lucy Sylvester?"

"Sure did. The woman is upright and moral. Inherited gazillions of pounds and made many more gazillions investing wisely and running a highly successful consultancy business. Why did you want to know? What's she done?"

"Nothing. She offered me a job."

"You'd do well then. The starting salaries at her firm are half a million."

"You what?"

"Are you thinking of leaving us."

"Nah. I'd miss you too much." Despite her words she idly wondered if Douglas and the kids fancied relocating to the States for a few years. Then she shook herself. There wasn't much call for a procurator fiscal in the states. In fact, there wasn't a call for procurator fiscals anywhere in the world except Bonnie Scotland.

"Thanks, Roy. I'll update you well when I return. Can't say much at the moment." Then she had a sudden thought. "What time is it where you are?"

"Six thirty." Then he added, "In the morning that is."

That meant it was one 1.30 am for her. "Why are you in work so early?"

"I'm not. You rang my mobile. Are you okay? You don't sound completely on the ball."

"I'm fine. Just exhausted. It's been a long day."

She hung up and the phone immediately rang again.

"McKenzie."

"It's Peter. They're letting me go. They've just said I've to rest for a couple of days."

"I'm coming to fetch you." She hung up and rang Matt.

Within fifteen minutes they were in a car and on their way to the hotel. Matt had insisted that they get some rest before writing reports etc. There was a fine balancing act between getting information down while it was fresh and being too exhausted to remember anything.

Despite the lateness of the hour Shona soaked in the bath before washing all her various cuts and bites. She then applied antihistamine cream to all the ones she could reach and swallowed a Piriton tablet. She'd come prepared.

Then she fell into bed and a deep sleep too exhausted to even think about making coffee.

Despite the fact she thought she would have nightmares for the rest of her life, she slept the sleep of the just.

She awoke to the sound of someone hammering on her door. She threw the covers back and staggered to the door. Peter stood on the other side, smiling and fully dressed.

"What on earth…" She tailed off and looked at him. What time is it?"

"Nine o'clock. Are you coming down for breakfast?"

"I'll see you down there. You start."

She showered and dressed in record time and joined him twenty minutes later. He was polishing off a plate of eggs and andouille sausage. She rather fancied that herself, so ordered a cheese, onion and pepper omelette and then took a pot of coffee back to the table before collecting the omelette and adding a couple of sausages to her plate. She also grabbed a plate of fruit to get some of her five a day in.

Silence fell until they had cleared their plates.

"We'd better get back to it then. Although you're meant to be resting."

"Aye. Well, I can rest just as well writing my report as I can loafing in a hotel room."

"Good point, well phrased." She thought for a minute and said, I'll have to book flights as well."

"It's a shame we'll no' get to do a wee bit off sightseeing while we're here."

"Are you trying to hasten the chief into an early grave. There's no way he'd go for that."

"Aye, a man can dream."

Matt and the team welcomed them like long lost family. "We hope y'all are feeling refreshed on this fine morning?"

"Fresh as a daisy. I suppose you'll want us to write reports?"

"Yes, Ma'am. Then I've set up your interview." He looked at her and smiled. "Well, two interviews I suppose, Miss Shona."

She frowned sensing she wasn't going to like this. "What interviews?'

"First Y'all have one with our Department of Internal Affairs." He took in the look on Shona's face and hurriedly added, "Y'all haven't done anything wrong. It's policy when firearms are used."

"Fair enough." She frowned again. "And this second interview?"

There was that dazzling smile that made Shona dizzy. "We're all going to be interviewed for CNN."

"When you say all, do you mean me as well?" asked Peter.

"Of course, Sir."

Shona thanked her lucky stars she'd worn a dress and decided she'd nip out and buy Peter a new tie.

The morning passed in a dizzying blur of bureaucracy, form filling and coffee drinking. Shona thought maybe she was really an American cop in a brit's skin. They drank even more caffeine than she did.

Before she knew it, it was time to be interviewed on CNN. They stood outside Police HQ where someone applied makeup to them all. Peter grumbled but took it for the sake of his five minutes of fame.

Then they were on air, reporting to the world.

"I have Captain Matt Hernandez of NOPD with me alongside his colleagues, Detective Inspector Shona McKenzie and Detective Sergeant Peter Johnston from Police Scotland."

Shona was pretty impressed she'd got all the names right. People in Britain struggled with it.

The interview went well but thankfully was fairly short as the heat was punishing. Although, the locals had jackets on.

The interviewer finished with, "Thank you to our Scottish colleagues for their service. Don't you just love their accents."

Back in the building a further surprise awaited. "Y'all are now officially off the clock. In gratitude for your service to us, you have three days to sightsee in New Orleans. Our superiors have agreed it between them."

"Wow. How exciting. Thanks."

Peter was grinning big enough for a brace of Cheshire Cats.

"And I've been given a couple of days off as well if y'all want a tour guide."

"We'd love one."

"Let's go grab ourselves some beignets and decide what we'd like to do."

Once settled in Café Du Monde with beignets and frozen chicory coffee they got on with the serious business of working out their tourist route.

"I don't suppose y'all want to do a swamp tour by boat do you?"

Matt roared with laughter at the look on both their faces.

"I never want to go near a swamp or an alligator again as long as I live," said Shona. "There's a special place in hell for people who like alligators."

"Me neither. Can we stick to dry ground with not a swamp, creek, or bayou to be seen?" asked Peter.

"We've got to watch out for Peter's heart anyway," said Shona.

"Don't go dragging my health intae this."

They decided after all the running about swamps the day before they'd start with a nice carriage ride around the French Quarter. They drove past buildings the carriage driver told then were called shotgun. "Y'all can stand at the front door and shoot a shotgun and it will go out the back door without touching anything but air on its way."

Shona thought that sort of stunt was a tragedy waiting to happen but contented herself with taking photos on her mobile phone. Peter did the same after she showed him how to use the camera.

"The wife would love it here. I might just have to bring her for a wee holiday."

"Good grief, she'll die of shock if you suggest taking her anywhere further than Loch Lomond."

"Aye, she likes Loch Lomond fine well. But she'd love tae see this."

Heavens, they say New Orleans changes people and they might just be right. She wondered if she and Douglas could come here for their honeymoon. Then, that got her thinking about whether they should be taking the children on their honeymoon. That sort of thinking gave her a headache, or maybe it was a lack of caffeine. She asked where they could grab a coffee to take away and drink while they wandered around the French Quarter on foot.

Matt turned out to be quite a knowledgeable guide and told them all sorts of stories about the place. The one about Delphine LaLaurie torturing slaves was horrific and sad. The grand mansion in which she lived still stood but no entry is permitted to the general public as it is now privately owned.

The three days flew past in a whirlwind of sightseeing. They went to the Audobon Zoo and took a trip out to a plantation. This was a place of both beauty and sadness. The mansion was magnificent but seeing the way the slaves lived brought the truth starkly to life.

They also went shopping and even Peter welcomed it.

"I want to buy carnival masks and beads for Alice."

"You may want to get a mask for the boy as well."

"Isn't he a bit old for that?"

"No one is too old for a carnival mask. Y'all can find him one he'll love."

They found a purple and gold one for Alice along with some purple and gold beads. Rory's was gold and black and looked suitably masculine.

Then it was down to the serious business of chocolate shopping. It turned out Matt was a guru on all things Hershey. They bought Hershey Bars so ginormous they could be classed as a lethal weapon, sweets, Reeses Peanut Butter cups and Jelly Belly Jellybeans. They piled the trolley so high Shona was beginning to get concerned they might not get it all on the plane. Still, she'd be their stepmother soon enough and she wanted to spoil them rotten.

She wished they could stretch the holiday further. However, it was not to be - Scotland and work beckoned. So, they packed their bags and reluctantly headed to the airport. Even the thought of seeing loved ones didn't make them feel any less sad. New Orleans weaves magic and holds a grip on you like no other city in the world and she had woven their magic on them.

Someone, somewhere had decided they should both travel business class which mean they had beds to sleep in. Shona, as she closed her eyes, and pulled the quilt around her thought she could get used to this luxury.

All thoughts of luxury quickly disappeared when they returned to Dundee. It was freezing cold with roads slippery with ice. She'd no sooner stepped foot through the office door than the chief wanted to see her with an update. She took him an Early Grey tea as an excuse to take her own coffee with her. About an hour later he'd exhausted all questions and she'd given him as much information as she could.

"Welcome back, Shona. I'm glad you're safe. The place hasn't been the same without you."

Shona was too stunned to answer immediately. Eventually she stammered out, "Thank you, Sir."

"I've had the deputy inspector of NOPD on the phone. She wants to award yourself and Sergeant Johnston a medal."

Could this get any more surreal. "That's very generous of her, Sir."

"Apparently she was impressed." He steepled his hands.

"Is that all, Sir."

"Not quite. After discussion with the Chief Constable, I want you and Sergeant Johnston to go for counselling."

"What? I don't nee—"

"You're going. No arguments. That will be all."

"Yes, Sir." Shona didn't have the heart to think about throwing him to alligators. That was a step too far.

The team were delighted to see them.

"Look at you with your suntans," said Jason.

"I'd say it's more mosquito bites than suntan," said Shona.

They outlined what had happened in New Orleans, leaving nothing out. The team looked a little pale around the gills.

"I feel sick." It would seem Abigail spoke for them all.

She despatched Nina and Abigail to break the news of Lola's death to Joshua's grandmother. She had a feeling she wouldn't be too bothered.

"Leave out the intimate details and just say she's dead."

She returned to her office to complete copious amounts of paperwork but first she rang Douglas.

"Shona, it's so good to hear your voice. Welcome home, my love."

As she settled back in her chair for a few minutes chat she thought, *this may not be New Orleans, but Dundee is definitely home.* She was home.

ACKNOWLEDGMENTS

Thanks got to the members of City Writers who have encouraged me and supported me throughout this books. Also for their excellent feedback which has helped me shape the book.

To Police Scotland who are so helpful with answering questions.

To the people of New Orleans for making my stay there so special.

To Jakki Parks Hatchett and Lisa Harris who I met in New Orleans and who are now firm friends. It was with them I first discussed this book.

ABOUT THE AUTHOR

Wendy H Jones is the award-winning, international best-selling author of the *DI Shona McKenzie Mysteries*. Her Young Adult Mystery, *The Dagger's Curse* was a finalist in the Woman Alive Readers' Choice Award. She is also The President of the Scottish Association of Writers, an international public speaker, and runs conferences and workshops on writing, motivation and marketing worldwide. Her first children's book, *Bertie the Buffalo*, was released in December 2018 with *Bertie Goes to the Worldwide Games* following in May, 2021, *Motivation Matters: Revolutionise Your Writing One Creative Step at a Time and Marketing Matters: Sell More Books* are the first book in the Writing Matters series. The third book in the *Fergus and Flora Mysteries* will be published in 2021. Her new author membership *Authorpreneur Accelerator Academy* launched in January 2021. She also produces T*he Writing and marketing Show* weekly podcast

She lives in Scotland where her books are based. She loves reading, travelling, and meeting new people, preferably all at once and is spreading her wings in this direction once more. Wendy also loves helping others to follow their writing dreams. She believes writing is the best job in the world.

Printed in Great Britain
by Amazon